"Your call, Cade."

The cop had the muzzle of a powerful automatic jammed hard against Janek's right eye. Other figures emerged from the front of the cruiser, their heavy weapons aimed at Cade.

Even if he'd been free and clear to take on the opposition, Cade wouldn't have put Janek at risk. There was no way he could take on the kind of odds facing him. Not now. He'd have to wait his chance.

One of the cops moved forward, his autorifle trained on Cade's chest. He reached out to take the SPAS, then passed it to one of his buddies. He frisked the Justice cop and relieved him of the Magnum. He grinned suddenly.

"Now we can relax, Cade. Welcome to Kansas," he said. Then he swung the butt of his rifle and clouted Cade across the side of the head.

The dawn exploded with brilliant light. Cade went down to his knees, feeling blood pouring across his face. The light began to fade, darkness rolled in like a heavy tide. In the distance he heard the cop's words echoing faintly.

"Welcome to Kansas...."

MIKE LINAKER

Firestreak

A GOLD EAGLE BOOK FROM
WORLDWIDE.

TORONTO • NEW YORK • LONDON
AMSTERDAM • PARIS • SYDNEY • HAMBURG
STOCKHOLM • ATHENS • TOKYO • MILAN
MADRID • WARSAW • BUDAPEST • AUCKLAND

If you purchased this book without a cover you should be aware that this book is stolen property. It was reported as "unsold and destroyed" to the publisher, and neither the author nor the publisher has received any payment for this "stripped book."

First edition January 1993

ISBN 0-373-63806-X

FIRESTREAK

Copyright © 1993 by Mike Linaker.
Philippine copyright 1993. Australian copyright 1993.

All rights reserved. Except for use in any review, the reproduction or utilization of this work in whole or in part in any form by any electronic, mechanical or other means, now known or hereafter invented, including xerography, photocopying and recording, or in any information storage or retrieval system, is forbidden without the permission of the publisher, Worldwide Library, 225 Duncan Mill Road, Don Mills, Ontario, Canada M3B 3K9.

All the characters in this book have no existence outside the imagination of the author and have no relation whatsoever to anyone bearing the same name or names. They are not even distantly inspired by any individual known or unknown to the author, and all the incidents are pure invention.

® are Trademarks registered in the United States Patent and Trademark Office and in other countries. TM are Trademarks of the publisher.

Printed in U.S.A.

Firestreak

PROLOGUE

Villas was getting tired of waiting for Brak. Just lately the guy had been getting to be a real pain, throwing his weight around as though he was running the business single-handedly, arguing with his three partners. It seemed, to Villas and everyone else, that Loren Brak had forgotten he had partners and obligations. Brak was always edgy these days, as if he was on drugs himself instead of just selling the stuff. Maybe the strain was getting to him, or maybe it was time Brak let someone else have his share while he moved on to some other enterprise. It wasn't as if he was all that happy about the Outfit's operations. He was always grumbling about something or other and was never satisfied.

Villas had known Brak for a long time. They'd all come up from the gutter together, pushed cheap dope when they'd started out, run a few girls and played the field until business took over and they realized they weren't in it for kicks. They organized, took on more territory and ran the business properly. Now they had one of the biggest independent drug setups in the country, with contacts and distribution running all the way to the West Coast.

But something was wrong. Villas knew it and didn't like it. Maybe that was what Brak wanted to talk about. Maybe it was why he'd arranged the meet with Villas at the Park Avenue apartment they used to entertain important clients and associates.

Even so, Villas was angry at the way he'd been kept waiting. He was a busy man and didn't have time to waste like this.

He shoved himself out of the lounger, ignoring the video playing on the holo-deck, and stalked across the spacious room. He paused at the panoramic window that looked out across sweltering New York. The glittering upper levels of the city, blurred in a shimmering heat haze, spread out below him.

It was the hottest August he had ever known, and he'd been through some of New York's hottest months.Turning from the window, Villas called for the housedroid.

The silver droid appeared and scuttled across the lounge. "You called, sir?"

"What's wrong with the air-conditioning in this place?" Villas snapped. He pointed to the vents in the walls. "It's blowin' warm air."

"I'm afraid there's been a malfunction in the central unit, sir," the droid apologized, cringing. "I checked earlier with maintenance. Apparently they have been unable to get the service company to send someone out."

"Great," Villas grumbled. "We pay all those damn charges on time and can't get help when we need it."

The droid silently watched him, aware of Villas's outbursts.

"Have we got any ice?" Villas asked hopefully

The droid nodded. "Plenty, sir"

"Get me a drink, then. And it better be cold. Understand?"

The droid smiled indulgently and returned to the kitchen.

Villas checked his watch. "You got until I finish my drink, Loren," he muttered.

He stared out of the window, watching an ad-drone cruise by. The drone's wide display was showing a sun-drenched strip of beach inhabited by bronzed, blue-eyed girls wearing nothing but gleaming smiles. The ad offered trouble-free vacations on the secluded beaches of the Spice Islands, while the stereo sound system badgered potential consumers not to miss the offer. Away from the daily grind. Away from the city's grime and overcrowding. And all for a small down payment.

Villas watched and smiled cynically.

The bastards never let up. Always on the make. Offering a way out. Something to take you away from your problems. But they never tell you that it will all still be there when you get back, with the added burden of the vacation loan.

He turned, his mind still on the nude figures, as the apartment door clicked and slid open.

"Hey, it's about time you showed your face. . . ."

It wasn't Loren Brak.

Villas didn't recognize the tanned, hard-featured man who stood before him. He was dressed in black. Even his gleaming hair was black, pulled into a pony-tail that hung over the collar of his leather jacket. Dark aviator glasses hid his eyes.

But Villas did recognize the Auto Casull. The massive stainless-steel weapon that took 454-caliber loads was leveled at his chest. The fist that held the autopistol was big and powerful.

"Who let you in?" Villas demanded. "This place is secure."

"Not when you got one of these," the intruder said. He held up a wafer of plastic that Villas recognized as a door card.

"Where'd you get that?" Villas asked. There were only supposed to be four of them, each held by the partners in the Outfit.

The big man grinned. It wasn't a pleasant grin.

"Brak gave it to me. He said to tell you hello—and goodbye."

Realization dawned on Villas. He had been set up by Loren Brak.

The son of a bitch *was* making his own move. By trying to take over the Outfit.

"No fuckin' way..." Villas screamed.

He snatched the autopistol holstered under his silk jacket, fingers closing over the cool, checkered butt, twisting sideways to present a slimmer target.

He felt the Beretta slipping free from the holster, curving out from under his jacket.

Then the Casull boomed with the thunder of an autocannon. A sleek bullet spun from the Casull's yawning muzzle, wreathed in smoke. It slammed into Villas's chest and exited between his shoulders. A glistening spatter of bloody debris hit the window behind Villas as he stumbled against the shatterproof plasglass. It bowed under the pressure, pushing him back into the room. Two more slugs knocked him across the carpet. He smashed into the holo-deck, tumbling across the path of the moving images. For a few seconds fantasy and reality blended in an odd mix, the phantom figures of the hologram shimmering over Villas's rolling, shredded form. Then he crashed to the carpet on the far side, kicking in agony.

The black-clad assassin put three more slugs into the twitching body. He holstered his weapon and reached into a pocket. He rolled some small objects between his fingers, making them crack, then slipped them into his mouth. He shook fragments to the floor, turning for the door.

The housedroid appeared at that moment, carrying the drink Villas had ordered.

The killer surveyed the droid, noting the tall frosted glass it was holding.

"Won't Mr. Villas be requiring his drink?" the droid asked, peering at the bloody form on the carpet.

The killer smiled. "What do you think?" he said politely, and left the apartment.

1

The driver's window on the department cruiser was jammed half-open. Hot air and the wail of the siren blasted into Cade's ear as he maneuvered the vehicle along the rutted, trash-strewn street. He was doing over fifty, hurling the heavy cruiser around burned-out wrecks and trying to avoid the deep potholes that broke up the surface. The radio was squawking continuously as the dispatcher tried to pull other available police vehicles into the area, and Janek hadn't quit grumbling since Cade had dragged him out of the Greenwich Village jazz club. The cyborg—or cybo, as they were popularly known—was a real jazz fan.

"If I wore underpants I'd have changed them three times already," Janek said solemnly.

Cade ignored his partner's moans. He was studying the street layout, deciding which turn to take next. This part of the South Bronx, a crumbling back lot of shabby buildings and filthy streets, wasn't his favorite place at the best of times. It had been a tough section of the city for years. Over the past five it had gotten worse. Very few people lived in this concrete wasteland through choice, and most residents were lucky if they survived more than a few months. The Bronx was a haven for the criminal fraternity. New York's lowest had adopted the South Bronx for their own, and most people figured it was worth the price to let them stay.

Cade threw the cruiser around a corner, bouncing it off the curb. Janek's head rapped against the roof. He turned his worst scowl on Cade, but the expression was wasted on the Justice cop. Gripping the wheel, he pulled the cruiser back on the street and floored the gas pedal.

"You got those riot guns loaded and ready?" he asked.

"Yes," Janek replied testily. He still hadn't forgiven Cade for pulling him out of the club right in the middle of a local combo's homage to the twentieth-century jazz great Miles Davis. The cybo had been waiting for weeks to hear the combo. Sitting in the near-dark of the club, he had been as close to complete satisfaction as he would ever get.

But his partner, Marshal Thomas Jefferson Cade, also known as T.J., had no appreciation for music, especially for jazz.

Sometimes his lack of appreciation and his habit of poking fun at his cyborg partner's logical methods annoyed Janek no end. On those occasions, or to get special attention, Janek would rather frostily call him Thomas, which in turn aggravated the rough-and-tumble Cade who did not like formality of any kind.

Although Janek was certainly in the mood to annoy Cade, he stopped himself from saying anything as the car shuddered with another sudden stop-and-go evasion tactic that made his teeth rattle. But at last they were at their destination, and shortly he would be able to escape from the roller-coaster ride.

The street ahead was blocked off with an assortment of police cruisers and SWAT wagons. Air cruisers and choppers flitted back and forth over the area. Uniformed cops, human and droid, had gathered outside the flaking facade of the tenement building they had blocked off.

Cade brought the cruiser to a slithering halt, throwing open his door. He flashed his badge at the first uniformed cop to confront him. "Who's in charge?"

The cop indicated a bulky man in combat dress and heavy body armor. "Harrigan. Local precinct commander."

Cade took the SPAS combat shotgun Janek handed him.

"Harrigan, what's the delay?" Cade asked as he reached the burly cop.

"Who wants to know?" Harrigan growled. Then he recognized Cade. "Should have known."

"Don't let it cramp your style," Cade said. He glanced around at the massed array of armed cops. "So why the waiting game?"

"Can't move until the negotiator gets here," Harrigan snapped.

"Still playing it by the book, Harrigan?"

"I don't move until I'm ordered."

"You know who we've got in there?"

"A bunch of drug pushers," Harrigan said, his eyes shifting nervously.

"You son of a bitch," Cade said. "What about the three Justice cops and Milt Schuberg?"

Harrigan shrugged, turning away. "They know the rules," he mumbled.

"Rules?" Cade yelled. He grabbed Harrigan's thick arm and spun the precinct commander around. Thrusting his Justice badge into Harrigan's face, he said, "My rules, Harrigan. I'm taking charge. Now move your ass out of my way."

"You can't push me around, Cade, fancy badge or not."

Janek, sensing the precinct commander's rising anger, quickly stepped in.

"Check your regulations, Harrigan," the cybo said evenly. "And don't be rash. You know very well Cade has the authority. Wouldn't look good on your record that you defied a Justice marshal."

Harrigan considered the cyborg's final remark. He was a cop who protected his own interests first and last.

"Okay, Cade, it's all yours. Official. Whatever happens is on your head."

"A good decision," Janek said.

The cybo watched the big man walk away. Harrigan crossed to a parked NYPD cruiser, shrugging out of his body armor before turning to talk to another cop.

Harrigan, I don't trust you, Janek thought as he stared after the man.

Cade had already collared one of the local street cops.

"How many in there, Frank?"

"We figure four, maybe five. Hard to tell. Milt went in to negotiate soon as he heard the perps had latched on to the three undercover guys. It all happened so damn fast. One minute it was just a drug bust—next thing all hell broke loose and there was a hell of a lot of shooting in there. I wanted to go in and help your guys, but Harrigan wouldn't let anyone move. You know about your guys in there, T.J.?''

"Only that three of our people infiltrated this bunch a few months back. They were trying to gather enough evidence so we could crack the organization for good.''

The cop pulled off his helmet, scrubbing a hand through his hair. "What can we do to help?" he asked.

"Forget about any negotiator," Cade said. "I'm not standing back and giving those perps the chance to carve our people up.''

"We'll back any move you make.''

"You got anyone around back?" Cade asked. The cop nodded. "Get them ready," Cade instructed. "On my word we go in and get this over with.''

"You got it.'' The cop reached for the mobile radio on his belt.

"You'll need this," Janek said, holding up the flak jacket he'd brought from the cruiser's trunk. "T.J., what do you know about Harrigan?''

Cade took off his leather jacket and dumped it on the cruiser's front seat.

"Not much. What I do know I don't like. He has funny friends, so the rumor goes. And I wouldn't feel good about him backing me in a dark alley.''

He removed the shoulder rig that held his .357 Magnum autopistol. Shrugging into the armored jacket, he zipped it up, then put the shoulder rig back on. Pulling the Magnum, he checked the weapon and cocked it. Then he recovered the SPAS shotgun and moved to the line of cruisers blocking the approach to the tenement building.

"How many windows they using?" Cade asked.

A KC-200 android patrolman pointed to a second-story window. "That's the only one we've spotted. We don't think they have the manpower to cover many more."

"Frank, I want your guys in there the minute me and Janek hit that front door."

"You got it, T.J."

Using the cruisers as cover, Cade and Janek crept to the sidewalk, then flattened against the building. The uneven sidewalk was strewn with trash, bursting plastic bags and rotting food. They stayed in cover at the bottom of the stone steps leading to the closed front doors.

Peering over his shoulder, Cade signaled to the cop named Frank and saw him raise the radio to his lips. Frank's sharp command reached Cade's ears, and he used it as his own signal to move.

He went up the steps at a dead run, shoulders hunched against a possible shot from the upstairs window. Janek appeared on Cade's right, and they hit the door together. It caved in, slamming back against the inner wall. As Cade went through the door, he felt dust and flaking plaster dropping from the ceiling.

The shadowed hall erupted with gunfire, slugs hammering the wall at chest level.

By this time the Justice cops were flat out on the dirty hall floor, the muzzles of their shotguns rising, seeking targets.

Janek's sensitive vision gave him an advantage. He spotted movement along the hall, in the shadow of the staircase, and lined up the SPAS on the armed guy leaning out of the darkness. Janek fired once, then a second time. The guy screamed, stumbled into view, his weapon slipping from lifeless hands as he crashed facedown to the floor.

Twisting, Cade picked up the hunched shape of an armed man easing down the stairs. His weapon glinted as he lifted it over the rail, aiming down into the hallway. Cade fired the SPAS, and the rail exploded in a shower of pale splinters, peppering the perp's face. Cade's second and third shots took him in the chest, whacking him back against the wall. The guy bounced, leaving a dark smear of blood as he pitched down the stairs.

"I'll take the stairs," Janek said, racing forward before Cade could argue.

Running along the hall, Cade heard the crashing sounds of forced entry as the NYPD backed his move.

Another gunman burst into view, throwing scared and angry glances over his shoulder. He'd come from the rear of the building. Too busy checking his backtrail, he failed to notice Cade, which was his mistake. Cade let him step close, then reversed the SPAS and clubbed him across the side of the skull. The perp slumped against the wall, howling in pain, his own weapon forgotten. Cade jabbed the hot muzzle of the combat shotgun against his throat.

"I'll give you five seconds to answer a question before I pull this trigger," Cade said tonelessly. "No one will ask why I shot you. Right now you're dead—unless I get what I need. Where are the hostages?"

The perp, bleeding heavily, stared up at the Justice cop. He was hurting already, and the SPAS's hot muzzle didn't ease his position.

"Look...I quit. Okay? No arguments. I ain't about to give you mothers the chance to blow me away."

Cade stared at the guy, unsure how to take his swift capitulation. Drug dealers weren't renowned for their superior intelligence, but they usually fought to the last man if cornered. Better to go down fighting than risk the chance of a stretch on Mars. Few criminals, however hard they claimed to be, relished the thought of working the penal colony on the red planet.

"You looking to make a deal?" Cade asked. "If I buy, it has to be top quality."

The perp shook his bloody head. "I just want out of this place."

"So answer the question. Where are the undercover cops? And the NYPD officer you grabbed?"

"You'll find out soon enough," the perp said, refusing to meet Cade's eyes.

Cade grabbed his shirtfront, yanked him to his feet and rammed him against the wall.

"If they're..." he began.

The perp held his hands up in a silent protest.

"T.J.," Janek called from the head of the stairs. "You'd better see this."

Cade shoved the captive ahead of him, forcing him up the stairs. On the landing Janek jerked a thumb over his shoulder, indicating an open door.

"In there."

Cade crossed to the door and peered inside.

The three Justice cops lay on the floor, bloody and torn, shot to death. None of them had a weapon in his hands. Cade stared for a long time. He knew each man personally, had worked with them all from time to time. They had been experienced, streetwise cops with a lifetime of knowledge shared between them.

"I'd say they were shot without warning," Janek offered

" 'Executed' is the word you're looking for," Cade said dully.

He moved into the bare, grubby room, vaguely thinking that it was a shitty place for anyone to die. As he moved forward, something crunched under his foot. Glancing down, he brushed the object aside with his foot and continued into the room.

Behind him Janek picked something up from the floor. He examined it carefully before dropping it into his pocket.

"Milt?" Cade asked. "He isn't here."

"He's along the hall," the captive perp mumbled.

Cade strode down the hall. As he passed the stairs he noticed the NYPD cops coming up. He reached the door of the room and booted it open.

Milt Schuberg, disheveled, with a large bruise on his face, was slumped in a chair. He was bound to the chair with lengths of plastic cord. He raised his head and stared at Cade with an angry scowl.

"So don't you ever knock?" he asked.

Cade leaned against the door frame, the SPAS sagging in his hands.

"You seen the mess we got here?"

Schuberg nodded. "'Mess' is the word, T.J. If the local cops hadn't come screaming in with sirens blazing, I'd be dead along with those three poor bastards."

"I got one of the perps alive," Cade said as he moved to free Schuberg. "At least we can sink him with the responsibility."

"You got it wrong," Schuberg said. He shoved up out of the chair. "The creeps here didn't off your boys. They grabbed me the minute I came in to negotiate. I got the feeling then that they were edgy. Like they were expecting something to happen. So one minute I'm sitting here, and the next thing I know the war's going on. I didn't know what the hell was going on until this bastard shows himself and points this handgun at me. Jesus, T.J., it was the biggest fuckin' thing I ever seen. He just sort of stands there, lookin' at me. 'I ain't gettin' paid to ice you,' he says. 'My deal was for the three Justice cops and the mothers in this joint. But what the hell . . .' Just then the sirens started wailing. Somebody takes a shot at this guy. He fires back, then takes off."

"Auto Casull," Janek said from the doorway. He held a misshapen bullet in one hand, along with several shell casings. "Took it out of the wall back there. I'd guess this was the standard .454-caliber load. They do make higher velocity loads for the Casull, but if those had been used we'd need to search the next block for the slugs."

"I said it was a big gun," Schuberg said. He glanced at Janek. "Can't be many guys around using one of those."

"I'll run a check," the cyborg said. "See if I can come up with anything."

"What about the shooter?" Cade asked. "You ID him?"

"Big sucker," Schuberg said. "All in black. Hair in a ponytail, pulled back from his face. Leather jacket. Wore aviator glasses. Had a good tan, the kind you have to work on under a lamp. Big hands to match his build. I didn't know him. He could be an out-of-town hitter."

Cade returned to the room where the dead Justice cops lay. Uniformed NYPD cops stood in silence around the door.

"I radioed for the ambulance," Frank told Cade. "Sorry about your guys."

"Thanks, Frank."

Cade went downstairs and out onto the street. As he walked across to the cruiser, he spotted Harrigan talking to a plainclothes cop.

"You can go in now, Harrigan," Cade said. "It's safe."

"The hell with you, Cade," Harrigan stormed.

Janek was locked to the inboard computer. His fingertip sensors connected him with the Justice Department computer. The cyborg glanced up as Cade approached.

"Can we talk, or are you having a micro-orgasm again?" Cade asked.

"Humor at my expense is a wasted effort, Thomas," Janek said with a smirk. "I refuse to rise to your baiting."

Cade slumped in the driver's seat, fishing a cigar from his pocket.

"Not even a small tantrum?"

"No."

"You're no fun anymore."

Cade lit the cigar. He leaned his head against the headrest, staring out at the feverish activity around the tenement building.

Janek broke contact with the computer and glanced at his partner. The cyborg obviously had some interesting information to pass along. Cade could sense the cyborg's mood as well as any human partner's. He deliberately ignored Janek, drawing heavily on his cigar.

"*You're* having the attitude problem instead, I take it?" Janek asked after a silent period.

"I am? Why? Did you have something to tell me?"

"All right, Thomas, you're funny. Okay. Ha-ha-ha."

"So what have you found?"

"While the computer was searching anyone who favors an Auto Casull, I checked to see if there had been any other incidents recently."

"And?"

"There was a shooting in an apartment on Park Avenue. A single male victim. Shot to death. The officers called in found shell casings on the floor that were identified as .454 Auto Casull. The dead man has been named as Antonio Villas. Cuban born. A known drug dealer belonging to the same organization as the men in the tenement building.''

''When did this happen?'' Cade asked as he fired up the cruiser's turbocharged engine.

Janek smiled. ''Less than three hours ago.''

There was a squeal of tires, and Cade switched on the siren before he cleared the cordon of police vehicles.

2

Cade had picked up Park Avenue Elevated-2 after driving across the Harlem River. He pushed the cruiser to the limit, leaving the decaying sprawl of the South Bronx behind, the elevated road taking them high above the city streets. In the deep canyons of New York the population sweltered in the cloying heat while Cade enjoyed the rush of air from the open window. He would have preferred it to have been colder, but he wasn't going to complain too much. He picked up the police marker beacon hovering over the plaza fronting the apartment tower and swung the cruiser off the highway. The wide plaza, decorated with ebony sculptures, was thronged with NYPD cruisers and the entrance had been closed off with barriers.

"Hey, Zack," Cade called to one of the uniformed cops. "Let me in."

The cop waved and activated the barrier. Cade drove onto the plaza and parked.

"We can all go home now, boys." The cop named Zack grinned as Cade and Janek stepped out of the cruiser. "The city's finest detective team is here to crack the case."

"Who's running this circus?" Cade asked.

"Lieutenant Dixon."

"He up there?"

Zack nodded.

Cade led the way inside, showing his badge to a uniformed KC-200 android on the foyer door.

In the elevator Cade glanced at his silent partner. "Something on your mind?"

The cyborg shook his head. "Not to do with the case."

"So you can still tell me."

"I find this difficult to discuss...."

"What? You got someone pregnant?"

"Highly amusing," Janek muttered. He began to study the elevator walls.

"Hey, partner, I'm still here."

"You'll laugh," Janek complained.

"No."

"I...it's Abby," Janek said.

Dr. Abigail Landers was in charge of Cybo Tech's New York facility. Janek had been visiting her following the discovery that his development had exceeded the expectations built into his electronic brain. Abby Landers, full of curiosity, had agreed to counsel Janek but to keep her findings to herself.

"So?" Cade asked.

"T.J., I've started to develop strange feelings where Abby is concerned. I find them hard to control."

"Hostility? I thought you liked her."

"I do. And that's the problem. The feelings are connected to the fact that I like her. It's odd, T.J. Sometimes those feelings make me happy, but sometimes I feel depressed. And I shouldn't be experiencing those feelings. I'm a cyborg, not a living being.''

"Hey, you'll handle it," Cade said. "Know what you just described?"

"What?"

"Being in love."

"I was being serious, T.J."

"And so was I. Just think about it," Cade said.

The car stopped, and the doors slid open. Cade and Janek stepped into the corridor. The apartment they wanted had a cop on the door. Cade showed his badge, Janek doing the same. They went inside. Although the SOC team had finished its work, the corpse was still in place, covered by a transparent plastic sheet.

A homicide detective was reclining in a bodyform lounger. He was black and in his thirties, with the kind of looks that would have netted him a fortune in the movies. He looked up when he became aware of Cade and Janek.

"So it's you two again," he said by way of greeting. Climbing out of the lounger, he took Cade's hand. "Been a while, T.J. How you doing?"

"Surviving," Cade said. "What you got for us?"

"Antonio Villas. One of the Outfit's top boys," Dixon said. "Way things have been happening today, I'd say we've got ourselves the beginnings of a gang fallout here."

"You heard about the mess over the Bronx?" Cade asked, gazing around the luxury apartment.

Dixon nodded. "I also heard you pulled Milt Schuberg out of the shit, too."

"Mind if I talk to the recorder?" Janek asked.

"Go ahead," Dixon said.

The cyborg crossed the room to where a short, bulky android was questioning the housedroid. The android had an NYPD emblem fixed to its upper chest.

"Marshal Janek," the cyborg said, showing his badge.

The recorder android scanned the badge's bar code, acknowledging Janek's identity.

"Can I help?" it asked. Its voice was smooth, bland, with no tonal values.

"Just give me a summation."

"Victim identified as Antonio Villas. Known member of an illegal organization manufacturing and distributing drugs within the state of New York and having connections with a trafficking network extending across several other states—"

"How did he die?" Janek interrupted.

The recorder android scanned its internal video and tape banks, making quick adjustments.

"Victim died from gunshot wounds to head and body. The majority of shots were unnecessary. The weapon was a Casull .454. Used cartridge casings were found scattered about the floor."

"You find anything else?"

The android considered the question, rapidly examining the results of its inspection of the room.

"Yes. A number of husks were seen. They were found to be from pistachio nuts. Of a variety found in—"

"That's all I need," Janek said. He swung around to face the housedroid.

"Did you see the man who shot Villas?"

The droid nodded its silver skull.

"Tell me about him."

"Tall man. Dressed in black. He had black hair in a ponytail. And he was very tanned."

"Thanks," Janek said, and turned away, smiling as he returned slowly to where Cade was inspecting the body.

"Why is he smiling?" Dixon asked.

"Usually means he's figured out an angle nobody else has picked up on. I call it his smart-ass mood."

"You feel like telling us?" Dixon asked.

"I'm certain now our assassin is Tate Jessup," the cyborg stated. "Out-of-state enforcer. Based on the West Coast, but he'll travel for a contract. Come up with his price, and he's your friend for life. Always wears black. Hair in a ponytail. Likes to sport an all-year tan. Favored weapon is the Model 4 Casull .454 autopistol. Jessup has a passion for pistachio nuts. Always carries a pack in his pocket. His failing is that he throws the husks around like calling cards. It could be deliberate. He's never been one for hiding in the shadows." Janek reached into his pocket and pulled out a few husks. "I picked these up at the tenement building. Near the murdered officers. The recorder here registered some husks on the floor near Villas's body."

"This the info you pulled from the computers?" Cade asked.

Janek nodded. "I wanted to see if it tallied with SOC descriptions first."

"I'll put a call for Jessup to be pulled in," Dixon said.

"Might be advisable to wait," Janek offered.

"Why?"

"Give Jessup enough freedom, and he might lead us to whoever's hiring him."

Dixon grinned at Cade. "Too damn smart, T.J. I was happier when all they did was serve drinks and sweep the floor."

"That's discrimination," Janek said huffily.

"You guys need anything else?" Dixon asked.

Cade shook his head. "No. Thanks for hanging on."

"Tell you what I'll do," Dixon said. "Request we try to spot Jessup but leave him alone. We'll watch his movements and see if he goes home."

"We owe you," Cade said. "I want the whole bunch responsible for those cops dying. Jessup was only the trigger. Somebody pointed him in the right direction."

MINUTES LATER, as they crossed the plaza, Cade tossed the keys to Janek.

"You drive."

"Where to?"

"Downtown. Bowery Row. I want to pick up some street talk. If there's a gang fallout going on, someone has to have heard something."

"Sammy J.?" Janek asked.

"If there's been a whisper, Sammy will know about it."

"If he isn't hitting the juice again," Janek muttered.

Cade dropped into the passenger seat. "Drunk or sober, Sammy's the best info peddler we've ever had."

Janek rolled the cruiser onto the down ramp, back to the elevated, picking up the feeder lane for the Lower East Side.

"T.J., one day we'll go looking for Sammy and they'll have him in a specimen jar."

Pushing the cruiser to a steady sixty, Janek pulled over on the crosstown link. He swung the cruiser onto the access for the lower ramp, easing through the maze of staggered down-lanes until he was back at street level and on the fringe of the Bowery.

Due to the escalating financial problems that had beset New York since the late twentieth century, many derelict areas were still being ignored. For as long as most could recall, the Bowery had been home to down-and-outs, vagrants and winos. It was the place where the desperate and the lost came when they gave up hope. On Bowery Row no one gave a damn who you were or where you came from. Here everyone was equally dispossessed.

Janek rolled the cruiser to a stop at the curb outside an anonymous grubby bar. He parked behind a battered Toyota Aircruiser.

"Count how many wheels we've got," Cade advised as they climbed out.

Janek activated the electro-lock, sealing the doors and the windows.

"I think we're being watched," he said.

"I'd be worried if we weren't," Cade said, stepping across the filthy sidewalk.

The gloom inside the bar was depressing. The smoky room stank of sweat, vomit and cheap booze. There was also the lingering trace of drugs in the heavy air.

From somewhere a Muzak HoloBox shoved out tired tunes and images from overused tapes. Cade ignored it all as he crossed to the long bar. A slow-moving bardroid was listlessly wiping the wet bar top with a grubby cloth.

"Get you somethin'?" it slurred.

Cade showed his badge. The droid's worn functions activated dully. It scanned the badge. Somewhere deep in its circuits a memory stirred, and the droid raised its scarred head.

"You want information, Marshal?"

"I sure as hell don't want a drink," Cade said. "I'm looking for Sammy J."

"He was in yesterday," the droid said, eyes brightening.

"Where does he hang out when he isn't in here?"

"Try the pool hall three doors down."

Janek was already striding out. Close behind, Cade heard the cyborg yell in anger. He burst out of the door to see Janek grabbing the arm of a lanky guy. The perp, clad in greasy denims and clutching an iron bar, was standing beside the parked cruiser.

"...and I suppose the bar's something you pick your teeth with?" Janek was saying to the unshaven perp.

"How the hell am I supposed to know you're cops?" the perp replied defiantly. He glanced over his shoulder at Cade. "Jesus!" he snarled. "You pricks always travel in pairs?"

"Easier to take you out," Cade said. "He holds you—I beat your brains out. In your case that could take a long time."

"Look what he did," Janek said, pointing to a scratch on the door near the lock.

"I was checking out how tough the paint job is," the perp said.

Janek plucked the bar from the perp's hand. "I suggest you beat it, Jack. Far and fast."

"Yeah? Hey, this ain't your turf, cop."

Janek smiled pleasantly. "True. But this could be your neck." As he spoke the cybo effortlessly bent the iron bar into a horseshoe shape.

The perp's face crumpled. He stared at Janek, realizing what he was facing, and decided he was on a losing streak. "Okay, okay, I got the message."

Janek let go, and the perp stepped back, both hands raised in defeat. Then he turned and ran.

"I'm ashamed of you," Cade said. "Threatening a citizen with physical violence."

Janek examined the twisted bar before throwing it aside. "Worked, though, didn't it?"

They moved along the sidewalk, stepping over the sprawled drunks and sleeping derelicts. The heat at street level was intense, shimmering off the sidewalk. It closed in tightly, filled with decaying odors.

"Does this place really smell as bad as I think it does?" Janek asked.

"Worse."

Cade shoved open the door to the pool hall. The interior, wreathed in smoke, was just as gloomy as the bar, and the air stank of unwashed bodies.

"There's Sammy," Janek whispered to Cade.

Following his partner's gaze, Cade picked out the man's hunched figure as he made a lazy shot across the scarred surface of a pool table. He watched the ball roll as if it was the most important thing in his life. He was alone at the table.

Sammy J. was a lean, washed-out figure in shabby, mismatched clothing. His age was indeterminate—he might have been thirty, or fifty, or somewhere in between. When he straightened up from the table, the yellow light catching his face, his loose flesh appeared to be carved out of old, cracked leather. His eyes told it all. They had once been clear and blue, but now, set deep in their sockets, they told his story better than a thousand words. All the misery and deprivation he'd suffered was mirrored in them.

"Sammy," Cade said as he reached the table.

Sammy J. turned to the Justice cop, his watery eyes trying to focus. He rubbed them with the back of a trembling, wrinkled hand.

"You tryin' to ruin a guy's reputation comin' in here?" he asked. His voice was dry and raspy, but there was a trace of the old humor there.

"Yours or ours?" Janek asked.

Sammy waved a loose hand at the cyborg. "Still runnin' around with the metalman, T.J.? What's wrong—can't you off-load him?"

"He's got too much on me, Sammy. Trouble with cybos is they never forget a damn thing."

Sammy chuckled dryly. "You want to take a walk with me, guys?" he asked.

They made their way outside, and Sammy led them into the alley beside the pool hall.

"So you got business for me?" Sammy asked. He fumbled in his pockets for a squashed pack of cigarettes, lighting one with shaky hands.

"I only deal with the best."

"I only give the best. So what do you need?"

"Antonio Villas got himself iced earlier today," Cade said. "And there was a raid on one of the Outfit's distribution houses over in the Bronx. Three Justice cops bought it in the raid. It was all the work of one guy. An enforcer named Tate Jessup."

"I heard the name. Works out of L.A. Nasty bastard."

"We figure there's a fallout going down inside the Outfit. Maybe somebody trying to take over. I need some info on it, Sammy. You heard anything?"

"I did pick up a scrap about Jessup being contracted. But the scam was thin."

"You can do better than that, Sammy," Janek said evenly.

"If the game's on the streets, I might be able to pick something up now. Give me an hour, and I'll have something for you." Sammy glanced at the tall Justice cop. "My word, T.J."

"Good enough, Sammy."

"Meet me here. One hour."

Sammy scuttled off, his agility belying his gaunt appearance.

"So what do we do? Spend an hour taking in the sights of the Bowery?" Janek asked scathingly. "My education isn't lacking so much that I need this."

"We'll take a drive. I need to talk to Milt."

"HOW YOU FEELING?" Cade asked.

Milt Schuberg's image wavered on the screen of the vid-phone. It was a bad connection. Maybe the heat had something to do with it, Cade thought.

"Fine, T.J.," Schuberg insisted. "Hey, you pick anything up?"

"Not yet. Did Dixon fill you in?"

"Yeah. We've got Jessup's rap sheet going through all the city agencies. The word is to maintain sight only. Trouble is we might get some trigger-happy rookie out to make his bones."

"Get his bones broken if Jessup makes him," Janek muttered. He was standing to one side of the vid-phone, but his words reached Schuberg.

"Listen, Marshal Janek, I'll back any of my boys against those KC-200 metalmen any day."

"Hah!" Janek scoffed. "But are you ready to put money where your mouth is?"

"Will you two quit this?" Cade complained. "I'd start worrying if I didn't know you liked each other."

"T.J., we've been checking up on Villas's three partners. You know what? The whole damn bunch has vanished. Crawled under their rocks and dug in. Even the dealers have gone to ground. The independents think it's Christmas. And we've been getting reports on a rash of homicides. First IDs have come up with a few names having dealt with the Outfit."

"This whole damn deal smells," Cade said. "Gives me an itch, Milt, and I can't find the right spot to scratch."

"Hey, give it time. It's early in the first quarter."

"Yeah, but you know me. I hate standing around waiting for the action to happen."

"If there's anything to find, Sammy J. will dig it up," Schuberg said.

"I'll call soon as I get anything," Cade said.

"Before you hang up, T.J., I got a message for you. From Frank Cipio."

Frank Cipio was the uniformed cop Cade had spoken to at the tenement building. Cade watched the vidscreen fuzz, then clear as Cipio's taped message was played through.

"Just a word, T.J.," Cipio said. The cop looked nervous. "Shit, T.J., I can only do this the way I know. I got a funny feeling about Harrigan. You know I never trusted him. After you took off for that other squeal and the word came over the wire that Antonio Villas had bought it, Harrigan got kind of upset. I guess I was the only one watching him. Anyhow, he scooted off along the street, heading for a pay phone like his pants were on fire. He made a call. Looked like he was upset with someone. Soon as he finished his call, he got in his car and rolled out. Maybe I'm getting paranoid, but the way he acted . . . well, it looked weird to me. That's it, pal."

Schuberg's face reappeared as the recording ran out. He stared at Cade. "What was that? Cipio's tape was for your eyes only, with an inbuilt wipe once you viewed it. You going to give?"

"Have to check something out first, then I'll let you know," Cade said.

He hung up, turning to survey the near-deserted diner. The place glittered with plastic and chrome.

Little had been done to alter the traditional decor of the uniquely American phenomenon, and even now, well into the twenty-first century, the diner didn't look out of place. The only distinct difference was the counterman. Clad in spotless whites, cap perched on the side of its gleaming skull, the droid exuded homely warmth and an eagerness to please.

"Give me another coffee," Cade said. "And a piece of that pie."

"Coming right up, sir," the droid warbled.

Janek visibly cringed. "I hate it when they do that."

"Cut it out, Janek. You know it's only working to its program. It's happy." Cade slid into the booth, watching Janek across the table. "All you do is gripe about everything."

"I have cause," the cybo pointed out. "How often do you think he gets shot at? Blown up? Raced around town in a car driven by a maniac?"

"When did that happen?"

"The last time *you* took the damn wheel."

The droid appeared with Cade's order. It placed the items on the table with smooth precision.

"You got the bill?" Cade asked.

The droid produced the bill. Cade paid, and the droid beamed at him. "Enjoy your meal, sir."

"Choke on your pie, sir," Janek muttered in perfect mimicry of the droid's voice.

"What does the gorgeous Dr. Abby Landers have to say about your moods?" Cade asked. "Doesn't it sort of take the edge off your cozy dates?"

"That isn't funny, Thomas," Janek snapped icily. "Deprecating humor is in extremely poor taste."

Cade grinned. "That's why I like it."

"Time we headed back for our meeting with Sammy," Janek said tersely.

Cade finished his pie and coffee, noting with concealed humor that Janek was allowing his impatience to show. The cyborg sat drumming the table with his fingers. That, Cade thought, was another one for Landers's file: a cyborg showing signs of stress.

"Let's go," Cade said suddenly. "Or are you staying here all day?"

The cruiser rolled through the traffic, with Cade changing lanes when the mood suited him. When the snarl of vehicles became too intense, he hit the siren and cleared a way through, ignoring the clenched fists and insults.

"That was good for public relations," Janek observed dryly.

Cade cut down a side street, swinging back onto the main drag and veering wildly around the rear of a massive city utilities vehicle. Water was gushing up from a fractured pipe just ahead. A team of droids, supervised by a human, was tackling the break.

"Goddamn city is coming apart at the seams," Cade grumbled as he powered away. His mood wasn't improved by the water that had sprayed into the cruiser through the jammed window.

He reached the pool hall with a minute to spare, parking just short of the alley.

"You stay with the car," Cade said. "Watch my back."

Janek nodded, reaching down to unlimber the loaded SPAS combat shotgun clamped under the cruiser's dash. He racked a shell into the breech and clicked off the safety, laying the weapon across his legs.

The cyborg watched his partner reach the mouth of the alley. Sammy J. wasn't in sight.

The radio on the dash muttered as a stream of police and Justice Department bulletins drifted through the airwaves. Janek's sensitive hearing was able to isolate and filter out the information he wanted to hear, blanking out everything else. He leaned back. The sun was warm on his face; his built-in sensors told him it was hot. Behind his eye lens a computer readout told him the exact temperature.

Focusing sharply, Janek picked out Sammy J.'s shambling figure approaching Cade. The info peddler stood close to the cop, his arms waving as he relayed his information. He could have picked up Sammy's voice with his hearing mode, but he found reading Sammy's lips a more stimulating challenge.

Janek's attention was drawn to a car rolling along the street. It was nothing out of the ordinary: a standard factory-line Ford in need of a paint job. The cyborg found it curious that it was moving at walking pace, as if the driver was looking for somewhere to park.

Or because it was getting into position for a run.

The vehicle accelerated, burning rubber as it shot forward, swerving onto the sidewalk.

The dark barrels of autoweapons poked out of the windows. As the car bounced along the sidewalk, bearing down on Cade and Sammy J   the weapons opened up. The air was punctured by the rattle of autofire. Concrete and glass filled the air as the slugs chewed at buildings, moving along to where Cade and Sammy J. stood.

3

Janek kicked open his door, sprang from the cruiser, swung the SPAS into firing position. He leveled the shotgun and touched the trigger. The barrel lifted as the first shot erupted from the muzzle. The blast took out the windshield and peppered the face of the gunner beside the driver. The stricken guy arched back against the seat, clapping his hands to his bloody face. The unnerved driver let his control slip, and the rocking vehicle swung away from the sidewalk in a deadly curve toward the parked cruiser and Janek.

The cyborg refused to give way. He stood his ground and fixed his gaze on the hit car, raised the SPAS and fired into the chest of the driver. The perp squealed, a high, cold sound, as his chest gushed blood. His body went into spasm, and his right foot jammed hard on the gas pedal. The out-of-control vehicle clipped the front of the cruiser, sending it slithering across the street. Janek, realizing he couldn't escape in time, took a long stride forward, then threw himself across the hood of the cruiser. He landed on his shoulder and rolled, bouncing as he hit the street on the far side.

The concrete around Janek exploded in a spray of geysers as autofire from the hit men in the back seat peppered the area. The cybo had the presence of mind to keep rolling as he hit the ground, barely managing to keep ahead of the marching line of slugs.

The heavy rap of an autopistol joined the melee. Cade had pushed Sammy J. aside, then pulled his .357 and drew a bead on the car as it swept by. As the vehicle struck the side of the cruiser, Cade laid down a volley of fire that ripped into the hit car. Window glass exploded in glittering sprays, and metal clanged. Altering his aim, Cade put a single slug through a rear tire. The Ford sagged onto the metal rim, sparks flying as it careered even farther off course.

Drifting across the street, it slammed into a parked van and came to a juddering halt. The rear doors burst open, and a trio of gunners spilled out, turning their autoweapons on the advancing Justice cops.

Cade took out the closest guy, laying a trio of .357s into his chest. The guy twisted around, slamming up against the side of the stalled car before pitching face-down on the ground.

Janek, up on his feet, laid the SPAS over the hood of the cruiser and triggered rapidly. He caught one guy on the run. The impact knocked the would-be killer across the sidewalk and face first into the wall. Crumpling as if his legs had been chopped from beneath him, he flopped facedown on the dirty pavement.

The sole survivor traded a couple of shots with Cade, then went down with a .357 slug through his left knee. He threw his gun aside, wrapped his hands around his mushy kneecap and screamed bloody murder.

Janek crossed the street to check the interior of the Ford. He found two dead men and a number of weapons. Satisfied, the cyborg approached the wounded hitman. Ignoring his protests, Janek took him by the collar and hauled him across the street. He dumped the guy against the side of the cruiser so he could keep an eye on him. Reaching inside, Janek put in a call for backup and a med-team.

Shaken, Sammy J. gathered his wits in record time. He pushed aside Cade's offer of help and stormed over to where the wounded perp sat.

"You miserable shithead," the info peddler yelled. Viciously he kicked the toe of his shoe into the perp's side. The guy rolled over, groaning.

"Hey! That's enough, Sammy," Cade said, pulling him away from the injured man.

"Enough, my ass," Sammy protested. "They were trying to kill us! Want me to kiss him?"

"No. I also don't want him kicked to death before I talk to him."

Janek took Sammy's arm and led him away.

Crouching beside the wounded perp, Cade lit one of his thin cigars. "You want to satisfy my curiosity?" he asked.

The perp eyed him with undisguised hostility. "That partner of yours is homicidal," he said petulantly.

"He doesn't take kindly to being shot at. Now stop wasting time. The para-meds will be here in a minute. It'll be too late then. Off to hospital to fix your knee, then a long trip to Mars for recuperation."

"Mars? What the hell you talking about?"

"Don't give me that," Cade said. "You know the penalty for armed assault. Minimum two years on the penal colony."

"There a way I can pull a stretch on a farm?"

"I need information. Maybe we can deal. You're out of it now. You've blown your contract. Nobody's going to rush in and bail you out. So make your offer."

The perp scrubbed a hand across his face. "Can I trust you?"

The Justice cop smiled. "Can you trust your mother?"

"You ain't seen mine."

The sound of approaching sirens caught the perp's ears. "So?" he asked.

"Why the killing? Villas? The tenement massacre and the other homicides we've been getting? Which of the partners hired Jessup?"

"Brak," the perp said. "Loren Brak hired us. He wants to take control of it all. Knock out his partners. Grab the syntho-drug formulations and head out to the West Coast. L.A. somewhere."

"And Sammy?"

"We got wind he was snooping around. Asking too many questions. So Brak figured if we followed we'd latch on to his buyer." The perp snorted. "Only we found you."

"You got lucky," Cade said. "Where's Brak holed up?"

"Hell, I don't know. He did all his arranging by phone. I only did a face-to-face with Jessup. We were hired to keep the New York end under control. Jessup's job is to bodyguard Brak and see he gets wherever he wants to go."

"I'll find him."

Cade rose as air cruisers hovered overhead. A white-and-red med-cruiser dropped to street level with a whine of air turbines.

"Hey, Cade, we made that deal?"

"I'll see you go to a farm."

"Little extra for you," the perp said. "Don't waste your time lookin' for Brak in town. I overheard Jessup talkin' to him on the phone. The way I figure it, they're gone already."

Cade rejoined Janek. The cyborg was giving details of the incident to the uniformed cops who had rolled up.

"We need to talk, partner."

Cade outlined what the wounded perp had told him.

Janek watched the perp being loaded onto a stretcher and pushed inside the med-cruiser. "Loyalty isn't too strong with people like him."

"He's nothing but a shooter, Janek. Paid to do a job. That doesn't buy much else. He knows he's on his way for a stretch. And he's on his own. So he makes a deal for himself."

"Sometimes, T.J., it's a real pleasure watching the way the human race walks all over itself."

"Don't go bitter on me, partner. Hey, what have you got to gripe about? Look who you've got for a partner."

Janek grimaced. "It looks like we go after Loren Brak, then," the cybo said. "My info on him doesn't make pleasant reading. Brak's a nasty piece of work, T.J. His sheet is twice as long as any of his partners'. My profile of him suggests he'll go to any lengths to get what he wants. Including murder."

"He's running true to type, then."

"We go after him?"

"Damn right."

Leaving the street cops to handle the scene, Cade and Janek climbed back into their cruiser. The vehicle groaned in protest as Cade reversed and swung across the street.

"We'll get hell when we get back to the department," Janek said. "This is the third car we've damaged in six weeks."

"It's been a busy time," Cade replied.

He gunned the cruiser across town, sliding into the jam of traffic on Broadway. The broad thoroughfare was almost at a standstill. There were too many vehicles in a city choking on its own inadequacies. In line with other metropolises, New York had failed to upgrade the road and transit systems. The influx of people seeking the mythical protection of the big city had put New York on a perilous path. New problems made the earlier ones pale into nothingness. There were simply too many people. Overcrowding was the norm. And the lack of space led to tension, violence and criminals. Ever ready to exploit their fellow humans, they moved in with promises of better housing, better life-styles, better drugs to ease the pain of living.

It all added up to one big headache for the authorities. And for the law-enforcement agencies who were, as ever, the front-line troops in the ceaseless war against the lawbreakers.

Cade, hot and sweaty, finally wheeled the battered cruiser down into the underground parking lot beneath the Justice Department building. Bringing the cruiser to a shuddering halt in a parking bay, he cut the engine and leaned back in the padded seat, staring through the dusty windshield.

"Thomas? Are you okay?" Janek asked anxiously.

"Just taking a minute, partner," Cade explained. He glanced at the cybo, unable to hold back the grin when he saw Janek's puzzled expression. "It's hot and sweaty. I'm feeling burned-out and sorry for myself. A human condition, Janek."

Janek eyed his partner suspiciously. "I don't know what you're talking about. Are you sure you're feeling well?"

"Yeah, fine."

Cade climbed out, slamming the door. As he turned from the car, the droid who ran the department car pool legged toward the cruiser. The droid's skinny legs wobbled as it pushed itself to the limit. Cade could see the disapproving gleam in its eyes as it scanned the damaged bodywork.

"Marshal Cade!" the droid called. "We have to talk about—"

"Marshal Janek can explain," Cade said, neatly sidestepping the droid. As he headed for the elevator, he heard Janek's groan as the droid cornered him. "See you in the office, partner," he called back as the elevator doors slid shut.

Stepping from the elevator, Cade caught the blast of cool air from the department's air conditioner and silently thanked the efficiency of the Justice Department. He headed for his office, passing members of the department, and rapidly became aware of the air of gloom that hung over the place.

He knew what it was.

The deaths of the three undercover Justice marshals would be felt by every operative. Harm to one marshal was felt by all, and three deaths in one morning would lie heavy on everyone's shoulders.

Braddock, the department head, caught Cade's eye and waved him into his glass-paneled office. Cade stepped inside and closed the door.

"I hate it," Braddock said. "Something like this. What do you say to people, T.J.? How do you make it comprehensible?"

"You can't," Cade said. "It happened and nothing can make it any less painful than it is."

"I guess so," Braddock said. "You got anything yet?"

"Right now it's in a mess," Cade said. "But we're starting to make some sense out of it. Looks like a takeover by one member of the Outfit. Trying to knock out his partners and grab the prize for himself.

"Antonio Villas was hit in the Outfit's apartment. Then there's the hit against one of the distribution centers where our undercover team was working. They were unlucky enough to be in the wrong place at the wrong time. Milt Schuberg almost bought it in the same strike.

"Descriptions of the hitman gave us a lead. Janek pulled a name out of his memory banks, which matched up to what we'd been told. Our hitman is Tate Jessup. Positive ID. I got that much from one of Brak's hired guns. He's contracted out to Loren Brak. So Brak is our maverick. Wants control of the whole operation."

"Got a line on Brak?"

"Coming up. I'll get Janek locked in to his computer banks. If there's any information around, he'll dig it out." Cade hesitated. "One more thing. It looks like we got a bad apple in NYPD. I need to confirm it but I'm pretty sure."

"Who?"

"Harrigan."

Braddock leaned back. "I want you on this fulltime. Anything you need, just ask. I've had it with these damn drug gangs fouling up the streets. I want this bunch out of business for good. The hard thing to swallow is the fact we lost three good guys just because some lowlife wants a bigger slice of a dirty business. They're all yours, T.J. Take 'em out. And that includes any dirty cop you find."

Cade caught sight of Janek passing the office. "I'll get back to you," Cade said, and left.

Janek was peeling off his jacket, grumbling. "That was a lousy trick," he said as Cade entered their office. "You know how I hate that damn service droid. It's like having a crotchety grandfather waiting for you every time you come home."

"Janek, hit those computer keys. I want every damn word that's ever been put down about Loren Brak, his partners and the Outfit."

Janek went through into his part of the office and slid into his seat. Flicking on the switch he activated his powerful computer station, watching the monitors flicker to life.

"Thomas?" Janek swung around to peer at Cade through the open doorway. The cyborg had picked up a mysterious somberness in Cade's behavior.

Cade's silence intrigued the cyborg. He walked back into Cade's office and paused at the desk, his arms folded across his chest. He watched impassively as Cade yanked open a drawer and took out a pack of cigars they were always arguing about. Cade stuck one between his lips and fired it up, then exhaled a cloud of acrid smoke.

"Am I missing something here? I sense an atmosphere. You'd think someone died...." The moment he'd spoken, Janek realized what the problem was. His instincts had failed to warn him. The cyborg let out a groan of embarrassment. "Oh shit!" he exclaimed, unable to suppress the words as they rushed to his lips. "T.J., I'm sorry, I should have known. What a dumb thing to say."

Cade scowled around the cigar clenched between his teeth. "You're right, partner, it was. But don't lose any sleep over it. It's the kind of thing I'd say. Jesus, pal, you're only human."

Janek leaned over the desk. "I'm sorry, T.J. You lost some good friends today. It must hurt."

Cade shrugged. "Well, they wouldn't expect me to sit around feeling sorry for them. What we should be doing is finding the creeps who did it. Brak and his hired gun, Jessup. Time we shut that bunch down for good."

"What else is there?" Janek asked.

Cade glared at him through the smoke, shaking his head. The cyborg never missed a trick. He seemed able to sense any mood change, or the fact that Cade had something on his mind. Like right now. He sighed, leaning back in his seat, and relayed the contents of Frank Cipio's message.

"Hmm," Janek exclaimed. "I told you back at the tenement I didn't trust Harrigan. What are you thinking? That Harrigan's on the Outfit's payroll?"

"Wouldn't be the first time a cop's rolled over. The longer I think about it, the more annoyed I get over the way Harrigan held the cops back from going into that building. Maybe he knew Jessup was inside. Maybe he was giving him time to do his job and get out."

"If that's true, you realize what it means?"

"Damn right. If Harrigan *did* delay the cops deliberately, he also allowed our guys to get themselves executed."

"Let's take this a step at a time," Janek said evenly. "Agreed?"

Cade nodded, and the cyborg returned to his computer and began keying in details. He remained hunched over the keyboard for almost half an hour.

Cade left him to it. He had his own leads to follow. He picked up the phone and punched in a number.

"Harrigan, we need to talk. Right now."

Harrigan's solid features scowled at Cade from the vid-screen. His eyes were the giveaway. They advertised the fact that Harrigan was scared. Something had unnerved him. He was caught in some trap of his own making and couldn't find a way out.

"We got nothing to say to each other, Cade, so get off my back. I got a job to do."

"But who for?" Cade asked quietly

"Look, Cade, I don't know what game you're playin', but I'm pissed."

"And you're sweating, Harrigan. It's damn near coming out of my screen. Now quit stalling. Either talk to me or I take this higher. And you know I'll do it."

Harrigan stared at the screen silently, his brain working overtime as he tried to come up with an answer that would let him slip off the hook.

"Don't even think of hanging up. I know where your office is," Cade suggested. He was taking a calculated risk, pushing Harrigan with nothing more to go on than Frank Cipio's suspicions and his own gut feeling. "Take your time, 'cause I ain't going away. Maybe you want to call your friends again. The ones you called from that pay phone outside the siege building."

"How did . . . ?" Harrigan blurted out, then realized he'd said too much. "Can't a guy make a call without everyone getting suspicious? For all you know, I was calling on official business."

"Paying for it yourself when you've got a radio in your car? What am I, Harrigan? A dopehead?"

Harrigan scrubbed a fat hand across his gleaming face. His eyes wandered, searching for help that didn't come. "I want a meet, Cade. Off the record. You and me. Nobody else. If I even smell a setup, I'm gone."

"You've got my word."

Harrigan nodded. "The Park Avenue Elevated. Under the slip road. Exit 6. You know it?"

"No problem."

"Thirty minutes, Cade. No fuckups. I'm comin' in armed."

Cade hung up. "And so am I," he said under his breath.

He passed Janek's door. "Hey, partner, I'm out."

Janek glanced over his shoulder. "Need backup?"

Cade shook his head. "Strictly one to one. Other guy's rules. I'll leave my location with the dispatcher in case I need help."

"T.J., be careful."

IN THE BASEMENT Cade climbed into the cruiser. He opened the dash cupboard and rummaged around, muttering to himself about untidy cyborgs, finally locating what he wanted. It was a touch-operated personal transmitter-receiver, small enough to be worn in his shirt pocket. He checked that the power pack was functional before stowing it away. On impulse he unleathered the .357 Magnum autopistol to see that it was loaded and ready. He made sure he was carrying a couple of extra clips in his leather jacket.

Satisfied, he fired up the cruiser's engine and coasted out of the basement, swinging around the building and into the traffic.

He arrived at the meeting place five minutes ahead of schedule and parked against a concrete support pillar. Overhead he could hear the rumble of traffic on the elevated highway. Cade lit a cigar and leaned back, his gaze centered on the rearview mirror.

He appeared relaxed but in reality he was checking and rechecking the area, just in case Harrigan was trying to pull a double cross. Cade had rattled the man, despite only having suspicion as the basis of his accusations. Harrigan obviously had something to hide, something that was becoming too heavy to keep to himself any longer.

Harrigan's dusty cruiser nosed into sight and rolled to a stop twenty feet from where Cade was parked. The Justice cop stayed where he was, deciding to let Harrigan do all the hard work. After a minute Harrigan's door swung open and the big man walked toward Cade's car.

Cade climbed out and met him halfway. Harrigan gestured, and they stood close to the graffiti-covered concrete pillar. He seemed to feel safer with the concrete at his back.

"Okay, I'm here," Cade said tautly.

"Real hard bastard, aren't you, Cade?" Harrigan snapped.

"Am I supposed to make things easy for you?"

Harrigan sighed. He checked the shadowy areas under the slip road as if he expected each corner to be concealing someone.

"I had no choice," Harrigan said suddenly. The words came out fast, unchecked. It was as if Harrigan had to get them out before they choked him. "I had to keep the cops out of that building. Someone had a job to do. I had to stall things."

"Knowing those three undercover guys were in there? And Milt Schuberg?" Cade took a threatening step forward. "And you held back from saving them?"

Harrigan, sweating profusely, shook his head. "You don't understand. Listen to me," he blustered nervously.

Cade lost control and lunged forward. His hard hands slammed against Harrigan's broad chest, knocking him against the concrete pillar.

"No more crap, Harrigan," Cade yelled. "One more protest about having no choice, and I'll retire you permanently. The game's over. You're blown, Harrigan. I'm going to enjoy writing your ticket for Mars."

Harrigan's beefy face paled as Cade's words sank home.

Mars!

The penal colony!

"You wouldn't, Cade. Not to a fellow officer."

Cade's eyes settled on him. Their cold gleam convinced Harrigan it was useless trying to talk his way out with excuses.

"I had no choice, Cade. Believe me, I really had *no* choice."

"Everybody has a choice, Harrigan. Those three dead marshals had a choice. They volunteered to work undercover. What they didn't choose was the way they died."

"That was a bad mistake," Harrigan admitted weakly. His options were falling quickly now, and he was desperately searching for a way out. "Listen, Cade, I wasn't lying before. I'm in over my neck—big gambling debts I could never pay off. So I took money from police funds to try and cover myself. The trouble was it didn't help. Next thing I knew, someone had bought up my markers and he had me by the balls. Jesus, he had it all worked out, Cade. If I worked for him, maybe he'd wipe out my markers. What else could I do? If he wanted, all he had to do was tip off the police commission and I was finished."

Cade stared at the man in disbelief. "And you fell for that line? Harrigan, the lowest rookie on the beat knows you don't drop for blackmail. It's a no-win situation. Once you join their team, it's over. Doesn't matter which way you turn. All you do is step deeper in the slime."

"Damn it, I've read the book," Harrigan said bitterly, "and I've bawled out enough people about caving in. But it's different when it's your turn."

"Who picked up your markers—Loren Brak?"

Harrigan nodded.

"How long have you been on the hook?"

Harrigan's massive shoulders sagged visibly.

"Close on six months."

"Doing what?"

"Running interference. Tipping Brak when anyone came too close. Delaying investigations. Losing information."

Cade turned away, trying to cool the wild, unreasoning anger threatening to explode into white-hot fury.

"And you knew about his takeover bid?"

"Yeah."

Facing the cop, Cade asked, "Any idea where he is?"

"No. But I do know where he'll hit next if he has the chance."

"Where?"

As Harrigan's lips began to form a word, Cade noticed a dancing red dot had appeared on Harrigan's sweating forehead.

Red dot!

Laser!

The warning screamed through Cade's brain, and he threw himself at Harrigan, shouldering the burly cop aside.

A chunk of concrete blew out of the pillar, spewing pulverized dust over Cade.

Someone was using explosive bullets.

"Down!" Cade yelled, clawing at his holstered Magnum.

Two more shots came, fired too hastily. They chewed more concrete from the pillar. Close by, Harrigan floundered in the dirt, looking scared.

The Justice cop pulled his .357 and flicked off the safety. On his knees he twisted around, searching the area behind them.

He couldn't see anything moving on the far side of the highway, but the line of low, semiderelict buildings offered the only place a rifleman could hide himself.

"Cade, you got to get me out of this," Harrigan demanded.

"You want to run that by me again?" Cade suggested.

"You know what I mean," Harrigan said. "I'm in your custody. You have to protect me."

Damned if the son of a bitch isn't right, Cade thought bitterly.

Another shot, this time close enough to allow Harrigan to feel the wind of its passing. The closeness was too much for the man. Harrigan scrambled to his feet, turning toward his cruiser.

"Harrigan!" Cade yelled. "Don't be a damn..."

The next shot caught Harrigan in the right shoulder. The explosive slug blew his arm off in a mist of red, spinning him around like a leaf in the breeze. He crashed against the pillar, slithering along the rough concrete before falling facedown in the dirt, where he lay kicking and screaming.

Cade, turning, spotted the sniper on a low roof, sheltered by the edge of a ventilation duct. As Cade's gaze focused on the roofline, sunlight glinted on the barrel of the shooter's autorifle.

Cade ran forward, his Magnum swinging on target. He triggered a swift 3-round burst. After his third shot, he saw a dark-clad figure pulling back from the duct, shielding his face from splinters of concrete. Still moving forward, Cade fired again and saw the figure lurch off balance as a slug caught his shoulder.

Cade activated the pocket mike and barked in his instructions as he headed for the highway.

"Cade. I want a med-team right now at my stated location. Man down. Hit by an explosive slug. Loss of right arm and still losing blood. I'm in pursuit of perpetrator. Possibly wounded and considered dangerous. I spotted him on roof of building across highway from my location. I want all mobile units in area to target the location."

He dodged across the highway traffic, the heavy Magnum in his fist. Hitting the sidewalk in a rush, he

raced down the alley alongside the building he'd pinpointed as the one used by the sniper. It was shadowed
and filthy, littered with trash and inhabited by the usual
sprinkling of vagrants. They pulled out of sight when
they saw Cade's running figure and the autopistol in his
hand.

The screech of tires alerted Cade as he approached
the rear of the building. Skidding around the corner,
he spotted a black Chrysler RamRider, its super-
charged engine howling at full revs. Burning rubber
threw up clouds of smoke as the low-slung hatchback
fishtailed across the empty parking lot, the driver
hauling on the wheel as he tried to bring it under control. The back end rammed a stack of discarded drums,
sending them flying across the lot.

A dark figure leaned out the passenger window, an
autorifle held in one hand. Because of the car's erratic
line of travel, the shooter was unable to hold his aim.
When he fired, the high-powered explosive slug passed
way above Cade's head, taking out a second-story
window, frame and all.

Crouching, aiming the Magnum in a two-handed
stance, Cade tracked in on the car's hood. He triggered two shots, punching large ragged holes in the
metal. The slugs whacked into the engine, causing it to
blow. As the power dropped, the driver, cursing wildly,
aimed his vehicle at Cade. The Justice cop held his position long enough to lay down more .357 fire. The
windshield starred, and the driver was almost thrown
into the rear as the slugs hammered his upper body.

Cade rolled out of the way of the stalling car. As he
gained his feet, turning, he heard the crunch as the

Chrysler hit the side of the building. The doors flew open upon impact, spilling the dead driver across the concrete.

The shooter, despite his damaged shoulder, shoved himself clear of the car. He propped himself against the vehicle, the autorifle wedged against his hip, his finger on the trigger. The autorifle fired once, but the slug went wild.

Cade returned fire, pumping two slugs into the shooter's chest and slamming him halfway back inside. The perp slid off the seat, his twisted, bloody body wedged against the door frame. He stared up at Cade, blood oozing from his mouth, breath coming in raspy hisses from a punctured lung.

"Somebody pay you for this job?" Cade asked.

The perp frowned at the cop. "You figure I do it for nothing? What kind of dumbass question is that?"

"Because the way you fucked it up, pal, you should give them their money back."

"Son of a bitch," the perp muttered. "You lousy son of a bitch."

"Ain't I just."

Cade picked up the rifle the perp had dropped and inspected it. It was a custom-made job, built for precisely the kind of contract the perp had attempted to carry out.

The wail of approaching sirens reached Cade's ears.

"Anything you want to tell me before they come to take you away?"

"Like what?"

"Who you're working for Why the hit on Harrigan?"

"Harrigan outlived his usefulness. And he has a loose mouth. We had a tap on his phone. The bastard was going to sing to you."

"So you figured to drop us both. Well, you loused up, pal. And Harrigan can still talk," Cade said. "You didn't finish the job, sucker. Harrigan's still alive."

"I hit him. Saw it."

Cade smiled. "Yeah, you hit him. Harrigan lost an arm. But he'll live and tell me what I need to know."

A black-and-white cruiser lurched to a stop yards away, and uniformed cops leaped out, guns drawn.

"Relax, boys," Cade said. "All taken care of."

"What about him?" one of the patrolmen asked after he'd looked over the perp.

"Call in a med-team," Cade told him and moved away.

"Where are you going, Cade?"

"I'm going to ride in with Harrigan. He's got some talking to do. And I have a feeling I'm going to enjoy listening."

4

Cade wheeled the cruiser into the shaded alley, cutting the engine. He watched the unmarked panel truck pull in behind him, then climbed out and walked back to meet the driver. The Justice cop hunched into his jacket, feeling the chill of the early morning catch him. New York might swelter during the day, but the dawn still held a bite to it, pulled in by the winds from the Atlantic.

Milt Schuberg closed the truck's door, shoving his hands into the pockets of his coat. "Jesus, T.J., dawn raids are fine except for the damn weather."

"Feels fine to me," Janek exclaimed, simulating deep breathing as he stepped out of the cruiser. The cybo, clad in normal clothing, stood grinning at his human partners.

"Janek," Cade said.

"Yes?"

"Shut up."

"Grouch, grouch, grouch," the cyborg whispered as he went to the trunk of the cruiser to dig out weapons.

Cade led Schuberg to the mouth of the alley and pointed across the derelict area.

"That's it," he said, indicating a four-story building surrounded by a high wire fence.

On the far side of the large complex they could see the rotted pilings of the East River. Mist drifted off the water, rolling in across the complex's back lot.

Schuberg took a long look around. The area was deserted now. A couple of years back it had been a busy section of the riverside business complex. Now, with subsidence problems threatening the stability of the buildings, the area had been abandoned because no one would put in the finance needed to repair the sinking foundations. East River Park, as the area had been named, was another victim of the city's decline.

"We could have taken this place out if Harrigan hadn't protected it," the NYPD cop bitched. "Christ, T.J., the Outfit must have been truckin' their shit out here by the ton. How many addicts does that add up to? How many poor bastards dead because of Brak and his friggin' partners? Okay, okay, that's all gone. But we hit 'em this time."

"Go get your team geared up, Milt," Cade said. "I want to go in now."

The Outfit's production and main distribution center was located within the complex. It had belonged to a video production company that had gone out of business a couple of years previously. Unable to compete with the stream of canned programs the L.A.-based studios were producing, the company had lost its customers and had left the three-story complex to rot. The complex had been up for sale since then, but since the whole area was going to ruin, there had been no buyers. The place had stood empty until the Outfit moved in.

The complex stood in its own grounds, surrounded by security fences, and had extensive acreage at the rear, where exterior scenes had been shot.

When Cade had returned to the office with the information Harrigan had given him during the ride to the hospital, Janek called up a detailed map of the site on his computer. He had printed off a copy, which he'd brought with him, and as Milt Schuberg's squad of NYPD hardstrikers gathered around, the cyborg laid it out across the hood of the cruiser.

"The power company pulled the plug on this place as soon as it went out of business. I made a check, and no one has been doing any illegal power tapping. So that means if there is any power, the traffickers are supplying it themselves. Probably installed their own generators. I suggest we take those out first."

Cade nodded. "One thing to remember. These guys are going to be nervous after what's been happening. Maybe Brak has hit this place, as well. If that's right they'll be ready to shoot at anything that moves. So don't be heroes. If they decide to get nasty, it's their problem and they take whatever comes their way. I want information. What they have in their files. Books. Computer banks. If we pick up live bodies, it's a bonus. But I'm not going to be too upset if we end up with a high body count."

There was an uncomfortable silence.

Milt Schuberg glanced at the assembled faces. "You heard the man, boys. This isn't a roundup. It's a hard bust. Justice Department rules. The kind of action you guys are always bellyaching about. So here's your chance to hit these bastards where it hurts. Don't embarrass me in front of Justice by getting religion.''

"That'll be the day, Milt," someone said.

"Yeah, Schuberg for Pope."

"You know something?" a voice said. "I like the idea of kicking some ass for a change."

"'Course you do, Yancy. It'll make a nice change from kissin' 'em.''

"Sounds very unhealthy," Janek murmured into Cade's ear. "Tell me, T.J., do all humans have these weird sexual preferences?''

"I'll handle the power cutoff," Cade said, stifling a grin at his partner's last remark. "Milt, when you get a call from us, come in fast. Have your boys spread and hit the building on every floor. Have your chopper cover the roof in case these guys have their own transport.''

Schuberg nodded and turned to his crew. "Weapons check, everybody. And do up the body armor. I don't want to be filling in insurance claims when this is over. Arnie, call up the chopper and tell 'em to be ready if we give the word.''

Janek ran a quick operations check on the radio mikes built into the flak jackets they were wearing. "All set, T.J.," he said, pulling on a baseball cap to cover his blond hair.

Cade led the way from the alley. He crossed the street and slid down into the dry bed of a wide, concrete storm drain that curved along the complex's perimeter fence. With Janek at his rear he loped along the storm drain until he reached the spot Janek had pinpointed

on the map as being the least exposed. He climbed out
of the drain, dropping flat to the ground, and inched
his way to the base of the chain-link fence. Janek rolled
alongside, and they checked out the back of the complex.

Mock-ups of buildings and streets crisscrossed the
back lot, most of them having fallen into disrepair
since being abandoned.

"This was where they used to tape that cop show you
used to watch," Janek said in casual conversation. He
was checking the fence to see if it was electrified.

"What?" Cade asked.

"You remember. The guy had this female partner
who always ended up with most of her clothes ripped
off at the end of each episode."

"Who, me? You got me mixed up with someone
else."

"Come on, T.J., you haven't forgotten that show.
You used to tape it if we were out. You sulked for days
if you missed a segment."

"The hell I did."

Janek snapped the steel links of the fence with his
powerful fingers, creating a gap large enough for them
to slip through.

"It was called 'Riot Squad.' Had the largest body
count of any show on air at the time. The public loved
it."

"Nah," Cade said. "I don't remember."

"Remember, I can tell when you're lying," Janek
cautioned.

"Generators," Cade said, changing the subject.

He did recall the show, if only because the actress had reminded him of Kate Bannion. The red-headed reporter was not only tantalizingly lovely, but her smarts and good humor provided the kind of challenge Cade relished in a woman. Since he'd been with her, he hadn't been really interested in anybody else.

The smirking cyborg broke into an easy lope, covering the open ground to the first block of cover. Cade followed, the SPAS braced against his hip, eyes scanning the area. He flattened against the plaster wall of one old set, feeling the structure sway a little. He reminded himself that the fake wall wouldn't do much to stop a bullet if a firefight started.

Janek pointed toward the rear of the main building. "The way down to the subbasement is across there. If they've installed generators, they'll be down there. No way they'll haul them any higher. Remember they have to have a fuel supply to keep them running."

Covering each other, they moved through the crumbling plaster sets, skirting areas of piled debris and abandoned machinery.

Crouching behind a low wall, they checked the open area between them and the basement entrance. The down ramp beckoned, seemingly deserted except for a couple of parked panel trucks and a sleek Toyota HyperRam.

"Hold it," Cade warned as he sensed Janek about to move.

Moments later an armed black guy stepped out from behind one of the trucks. He carried a powerful Heckler & Koch submachine gun, fitted with a laser sight and extended magazine. Cade recognized the autoweapon as the latest model. It was capable of rapid fire, using high-velocity caseless rounds. The H&K was on the banned list for civilian use, but no one had told the gunrunners they weren't supposed to import it.

"Nice hardware," Janek observed. "If they've all got those, we could be in for a busy time."

"You should take up party pooping as a business," Cade said.

He flicked on his mike set. "Milt, you read me?"

"Yeah," Schuberg's voice whispered in his ear.

"We spotted one guy. Just passing this for your info. He's carrying the new H&K auto. Maxi-mag and laser sight."

"Shit, those things can chop a guy in half faster than he can say goodbye to his asshole. Where the hell did they get those things?"

"Ask U.S. Customs," Cade suggested.

"Thanks for the tip, T.J., we'll watch ourselves."

Cade cut the connection, tapping Janek on the shoulder. "We need this one taken out nice and quiet," he said.

"Do tell," the cybo remarked. He laid his weapons on the ground, slipping out of his flak jacket.

"Can you handle this?" Cade asked.

Janek stared at him from under the peak of his cap. "On a bad day without even trying," he said.

Working his way to the far end, Janek vaulted the low wall, breaking into a run. His speed increased as he poured on the power, his sleek form becoming almost a blur. He had skirted the periphery of the guard's vision, moving in a wide curve that brought him into the cover of the parked panel trucks. The guard turned at the last moment, seeing some flicker of movement. By then he was already out of the game, though he didn't know it.

Cade saw Janek slip behind the guard. His left hand clamped over the guy's mouth to silence him. His right locked around the guard's taut throat, fingers closing with inflexible finality. The black guy gave a convulsive twitch, then went totally limp. Janek held him inches off the ground, raising his left hand to signal Cade in.

By the time Cade reached him, Janek had the dead guy stowed inside one of the two panel trucks. Turning his attention to the vehicles, Janek raised the hoods and ripped out wiring, leaving the trucks and the Toyota out of action.

Cade handed Janek his gear. The cybo got into it as they moved down the ramp into the basement parking area.

The area was devoid of vehicles. The wide expanse of stained concrete stretched beneath the building. Janek paused in midstride, his head turned sideways as he searched for distant sounds.

"That way, T.J. I can hear the generator."

They moved from one support pillar to another, pushing deeper into the basement parking area. After a while Cade was able to hear the subdued pulse coming from the generator.

It was a large one, the size of a panel truck, mounted on a low trailer. Next to it was a portable tank, feeding diesel fuel into the generator's power plant. A thick cable snaked across the floor, vanishing into a room with a steel door. This was the power cable feeding the electrical circuit boards. A thicker, flexible tube trailed from the generator's power plant, taking away the fumes.

A couple of armed guards lounged nearby, keeping a watch over the generator. They wore ear protectors against the generator's chugging power plant. The protectors also drowned out the sound of Cade and Janek's approach. The guards were startled when they felt hard gun muzzles jammed into their ribs. But there wasn't a thing they could do. The Justice cops disarmed and quickly cuffed the pair.

Cade handed Janek one of the H&Ks, taking the other for himself. "Knock that generator off, Janek," Cade said. "And make sure it won't start again."

The moment the generator's power fell silent, Cade keyed his mike. "Milt, it's a go," he said when Schuberg responded. "We're going in from the basement."

Janek turned away from the generator, tossing a chunk of hardware across the floor.

He followed Cade to the door marked Stairs To All Floors.

They went up with their weapons cocked and ready for the resistance they knew would come.

"Hey! Who the hell is it?" a voice demanded.

"Who do you think—Santa Claus?" Cade asked, triggering the SPAS at the shadowy figure aiming an autoweapon at him.

The blast lifted the guy off his feet and spread him against the wall. Slugs from the autoweapon peppered the floor and ceiling in wild arcs. The sound ceased as the guy crashed facedown on the floor, his bleeding body twitching.

"Read him his rights?" Janek asked as he stepped over the body.

On the next landing they almost collided head-on with a trio of armed hardguys. The closeness didn't allow for weapons to be brought into play.

Cade swung the SPAS in a vicious arc, clouting the nearest opponent across the side of the face. The guy grunted with shock, rolling back against the wall, losing his grip on the H&K he was carrying. Cade closed in and whacked him a second time, then grabbed him by the collar. He hauled the dazed guy across the landing, spinning him over the guardrail. The thug fell out of sight, emitting a short scream before he landed.

In the same heartbeat of time Janek slammed shoulder first into the closest adversary. The guy was big and broad, with a wide chest. Even so, he was driven off balance by Janek's bone-crunching body slam.

Sensing the last man closing in, Janek threw a hard backhand. His fist sledged into the guy's face, breaking bone and dropping him where he stood. Turning slightly, Janek met the big guy's rush. The man had recovered quickly, but he made the fatal error of returning to the fight, unaware of who he was tangling with. His wild right swing was caught in Janek's fist. The cyborg yanked the man forward, head-butting him. The big man's eyes rolled up into his skull as his body shut down in the wake of the terrific impact. He was dead before his bulk hit the landing.

Cade kicked the door, slamming it against the inside wall. He went through, Janek close behind, and found himself in a long, carpeted corridor. The floor was littered with empty food cartons and drink cans. The traffickers had brought chaos to the once luxurious building. Wall decorations were torn and stained. The floor was dotted with crumpled sleeping bags and even portable TV sets, evidence that the factory had been in operation for some time.

Raised voices greeted the Justice cops as they barreled into the corridor.

Janek picked up the first sign of movement as an armed trafficker burst from one room into the corridor. The trafficker's H&K opened fire, filling the corridor with streams of slugs. Like most of his kind, the trafficker liked the feel and power of the weapon, but he was no trained gunner and he sprayed the area in an uncontrolled burst. The slugs went everywhere but at their intended targets, chewing holes in the walls and ceiling.

There was no sloppiness about Janek's reply. He leveled the SPAS and pulled the trigger in a smooth, unbroken motion. The blast from the shotgun took the guy in midchest, kicking him yards back along the corridor, trailing long streamers of bloody debris from the cavity in his body. He cartwheeled against the wall, twisting and turning, already dead but still on his feet.

"Keep moving, T.J.," Janek yelled, turning to lay a shot in the skull of another armed perp who stuck his head out into the corridor.

Cade, aware of their exposed position, fired at everything that moved, his tightly spaced shots dropping target after target. Together the Justice cops moved along the corridor, working as one, clearing the way around them with deadly precision.

They reached the double doors that appeared to be the center of activity. Janek shouldered the doors wide open, ducking as he went in. His sensors picked up rapid movement within the room, and he acted accordingly, knowing that Cade would be on his heels.

The wide, low-ceilinged room was filled with furniture and wooden tables holding a number of computer setups. Across the room were rows of filing cabinets.

There was also a trio of gun-wielding traffickers, screaming orders at each other as they turned their weapons on the pair of cops. Janek moved aside, his keen senses allowing him to anticipate the responses of the traffickers. Even as he moved, he triggered the shotgun and knocked one guy down with a single shot.

Cade dropped to one knee, lifting his own SPAS. He fired twice, each shot for a different target. The traffickers were driven to the floor in a split second, bodies torn to bloody shreds by the power of the combat weapon.

As Cade moved deeper into the room, checking it out for concealed traffickers, Janek slammed the doors shut. The cyborg scanned the room swiftly. "Looks like we got the jackpot."

Cade was already dragging open the drawers of the filing cabinets. He rifled through the papers inside, tossing some of them to the floor. "Somebody has been through these already," he grumbled. "Seems you were right, partner. Brak has already paid this place a visit."

"Take a look at the computers," Cade continued, still checking the room over.

Janek crossed to the line of computers. He laid down his SPAS and bent over the machines, keying in commands. He smiled as codes began to flit across the monitors. Janek liked nothing better than a challenge. He dragged up a seat and hunched over one of the keyboards, his fingers working swiftly as he tapped in deep-search commands.

Minutes passed as Cade searched the room from end to end. He found nothing of interest, convincing himself that Brak had stripped the place of any useful information. If there was anything left, it would be secreted somewhere within the microchips of the computers.

"Anything?" he asked Janek.

The cyborg nodded. "There's something in here, T.J.," he said. "I just need to break the codes."

Cade crossed to the doors as he heard the thunder of feet in the corridor. Milt Schuberg's voice rose above the din. Cade dragged open the doors and identified himself.

"Hey, T.J." Schuberg grinned. His face was flushed and beaded with sweat. "Damned if we didn't do it. Cleared the whole place. There's a manufacturing setup on the floor below. All geared up to make that synthetic shit they're peddling these days. Thing is the damn place has been trashed. Everything destroyed."

"Call in your cleanup squads, Milt," Cade said. "Sweep this place out."

"You guys get anything?" Schuberg asked, poking his head into the room. He spotted Janek and peered over his shoulder. "Picked anything up?"

"Only interference," Janek muttered icily.

Schuberg was too high on success to notice the sarcasm in the cyborg's words.

"Any survivors?" Cade asked.

"Couple of walking wounded," Schuberg said with a trace of regret in his voice. "They look well pissed off, T.J. I don't think we're the first bunch to hit them. Brak's been here before us. Probably wanted to get his hands on the goodies before he quit town."

"We left a pair cuffed down in the basement. They were baby-sitting the generator before we busted in and shut it down."

Schuberg glanced at the computer bank, then back at Cade. "How come...?" he began.

"The computers have their own power packs," Cade explained. "They're being charged up all the time the power is on. If the power's cut, the packs cut in and stop the computers going down. There's enough power in them to run for six or seven hours."

Schuberg shook his head in admiration. "Jeez," he said. "These designers think of everything. What next, huh?"

"I hear they're going to invent something called the human brain," Janek said very softly, just loud enough for Cade to hear.

"You want to show me this lab?" Cade asked, and followed Schuberg out of the room, closing the doors so that Janek could have the place to himself.

THIRTY MINUTES LATER Cade rejoined the cyborg. Schuberg was busy with his cleanup squads. The android teams were cataloging every item in the building, then ferrying them out to waiting police vehicles for transfer to the central evidence vaults in the basement of the Federal Building.

Janek was still seated at the keyboard. He had finished tapping in information. The fingers of his right hand were resting on the keyboard's sensor pads. Janek was drawing in the computer information through the sensors located beneath the skin of his own hand. He directed the electrical impulses into his own memory banks. Once there, they were permanent and on instant recall.

"The memory banks had been cleared," Janek said. "Somebody came in and wiped them. Probably took a copy on disk first. Thing is that whoever set up the program installed a command that had the computer retain all information in what they call a limbo file. As far as anyone could tell, the memory had been wiped. But actually the data had been hidden in a lost file with no way to get it back unless you knew the code."

"And you worked out the code?"

"Naturally. I'm a distant cousin to the computer, remember. I speak its language on its own terms, not as a human keying in requests. So I can reason with it and get it to tell me the code sequence without initiating any wipe messages. It isn't difficult, T.J. It's no harder than talking to you and getting you to admit your faults."

"Okay, Einstein, what did you dig up?" Cade asked, fishing out a cigar. He was vaguely aware that he found himself smoking the things whenever he and Janek had one of their heart-to-heart talks and the cyborg won hands down. The thought worried him a little.

"We've got a number of things here," Janek explained. "The formulation for the synthetic hallucinogenic drug the traffickers have been making. The formula is quite simple, rudimentary, in fact. But it creates an easily produced and powerful drug in crystal form. Thunder Crystals is its street name. Next we have contacts and drop-off points running from New York all the way to L.A. Our traffickers have been expanding. T.J., if Brak runs true to form, these contacts could be next on his hit list. If he's building his own network, he'll want his own people in place, not people loyal to the Outfit. If I was in his place, it's what I'd do."

"Same here," Cade admitted. He stared at the screen. "Harrigan mentioned something else during our little heart-to-heart. He was vague, but his suggestion was there are some high-powered financiers involved. Money men in the city. Harrigan figured these guys were in it for the fast money. If it's true, they're probably helping to launder the traffickers' cash. We need something hard to tie them in with the traffickers."

"Maybe this," Janek said, bringing a fresh set of figures to the monitor.

Cade stared at the tangled overlay of figures, numbers and symbols. "What the hell is that?"

"I'd say a mixed code of some kind," Janek explained. "Somebody decided to add a second security lock on the information. Could be we've got something juicy in among that mess. Deposit box numbers maybe. Account numbers. Take your pick. It might be the link we need to pin down these money men supposedly backing the Outfit, or it could just be a dead end."

"Can you sort it out?"

"Maybe," the cybo said. "It's an oddball coding. Never seen anything like it before."

"Man or machine code?"

Janek's shoulders rose in his imperfect shrug. "I'd say machine code, but don't quote me. Whatever, it's going to take some breaking."

"Can you do it?"

"I can try. I've got it up here," Janek said, tapping the side of his head. "I'll keep trying."

"Okay, partner, we're out of here. I want Loren Brak behind bars. He might have started this mess— but I'm damn certain I'm going to finish it."

"We need a starting point, T.J. I've got a suggestion."

"Go ahead. I'm open to offers."

Janek tapped the monitor. "Here. Mid Town, Kansas. There's information on a company called Mid State. Big freighting company town. Focal point for distribution of goods to all points. Has the railroad passing through. Ideal place for drug distribution."

"We'll run a check on the place," Cade said. "If it shows promise, we'll take a look."

5

Cade sat facing Braddock across the commander's wide desk. The meeting had been at Braddock's insistence. He was becoming worried the way the situation was developing, and in his usual blunt manner he laid it on the line for the Justice cop.

"It's like a war's erupted out there. The body count is going up by the minute."

Braddock tossed a stack of report sheets across the desk for Cade to scan. "Hit-and-run raids in half a dozen locations. Officers in attendance have reported they've been faced by drug-distribution setups. Vehicle stores. Even a damn armory. And bodies everywhere they go. All belonging to the Outfit. There have also been attacks on homes belonging to Lorenzo and Shultz. This time it was only damage to the properties because that pair has vanished. No sight of them anywhere. I figure they've gone underground. Brak has put the fear of God in the whole outfit."

Cade returned the reports. "He's been cutting down the opposition. Breaking up the Outfit. He's causing as much confusion as he can to take the heat off him while he cuts and runs."

"T.J., I want that mother. Dead or alive, I want him out of harm's way. Brak has a big bill to pay, and top of the list are our three guys. You can call this personal if you want, but I want Brak."

"You and me both," Cade said. "We're ready to roll. Janek's down in the armory right now, picking up weapons. There's just one more thing I need."

"Name it."

"A chopper. If Brak's heading cross-country, I want something we can track him with. And something that moves fast."

Braddock picked up his phone, punched in a number, stared at the screen. "Bert, I want our best pursuit chopper fueled up and ready to go in thirty. Full complement of equipment, and make sure the damn thing is armed to the teeth. Call T.J. when it's ready."

"I'll go see if Janek's got anything from that info he got from the Outfit's computer."

"You really think there's going to be anything worth salvaging from it?"

Cade shrugged. "Can't be certain. But why go to all the trouble of hiding it and scrambling a special code if it's useless junk?"

"How the hell would I know? You're the detective. Hey, maybe it was done as a deliberate stall to waste our time."

Cade grinned. "No way. Janek can decipher it while he's flying."

"Flying what, T.J.?"

Janek stood in the doorway, listening. He was dressed in a black one-piece combat suit similar to Cade's. He also wore combat boots.

"We're going after Brak," Cade said. "In a chopper. Your name came up as pilot."

"Thanks for giving me the choice."

Braddock stood. "You got anything out of that spaghetti, Janek?"

Janek glanced at Cade, unsure what Braddock meant.

"Nothing to do with food, partner. The boss wants to know if you've decoded that computer info yet."

"It's taking a little longer than I anticipated," the cyborg said. "But I'll get there."

"That'll do for me. Just watch your backs, fellas. But take out these mad dogs before they kill half the population."

"On our way," Cade said. "First stop Mid Town, Kansas. I'm betting on that being the first stop on Brak's list. He'll want to dump anyone who doesn't want to join his new setup."

There was a stack of weaponry on Cade's desk. He checked it over, smiling at Janek's choice. The cyborg, using his inbuilt logic, had gone for a selection of weapons to cover all emergencies. Alongside compact autoweapons were long-range rifles fitted with laser sights and expanded magazines. The autorifles, precision weapons designed for the military, were some of the best U.S.-made firearms available. Janek had also brought along grenades: stun, explosive and gas. Additional handguns lay next to flak jackets and a pair of carbon-steel combat knives.

"Enough?" Janek asked.

If we're aiming to fight a war," Cade remarked.

Janek hefted a couple of ammunition boxes. "I'll get these up to the roof."

Cade sat down and punched in a number on the vid-phone. He watched the screen fuzz, then blur. He shook his head in annoyance. The heat wave was playing havoc with the transmission signals.

He tried the number again. This time the vid-phone hiccuped, and Kate Bannion's lovely face filled the screen. She smiled when she recognized Cade.

"Hi, T.J.," she said.

"I'm going out of town for a while," Cade said.

"Going to tell me why?"

"You heard about the gang killings?"

"You must be joking. They're all we've been hearing about. Shootings. Murder. Destruction. What is going on in this town, T. J. Cade?"

"One guy wanting to get rid of his partners so he can run the whole business himself."

"Loren Brak?"

"Been doing your homework."

"Sure. I'm a good reporter. But you already know that. Brak had three partners, right? Villas. Lorenzo. Shultz. Villas is dead. My sources tell me Lorenzo and Shultz have run for the hills. Nobody knows where they are."

"What other information have you picked up?"

"I heard a whisper that Loren Brak has quit the city. He's vanished. Picked up his bags and gone."

Cade grinned.

"Damn it, T.J., that's where you're going, isn't it? After Brak. Has to be you. Doesn't anybody else in your department do any dirty work?"

"Three of them did," Cade said soberly. "And you know what happened to them."

Kate nodded. "That was terrible, T.J."

"They were slaughtered like cattle," said Cade.

"Any idea by whom?"

"We've got a name. A hired gun called Tate Jessup. Doing Loren Brak's dirty work."

Kate stared at him for a while. "T.J., be careful. How long will you be away?"

"Can't say. We have to find Brak before we can stop him."

"Call me if you can. I'm hunting down a promising story now, but I'll keep my ears open and I'll pass along anything I can."

"Will do, but I think this will be just a race to see who gets first to the finish line. If I can't call, don't fret, babe."

Concern showed in her green eyes, and she began to speak. Just at that moment the vid-screen fuzzed over, and Kate's image broke up. Her words were lost in a crackle of static. Cade heard something that sounded like *love* but he couldn't be sure.

The screen went blank. A text message apologized for the service breakdown. Cade slammed the receiver down with a growl of anger, staring at the gray, dead screen with mounting disgust.

"Lousy technology," he muttered bitterly.

He dropped the phone and snatched up his jacket. Without a backward glance Cade made for the elevator and the helipad on the roof, where Janek was waiting for him.

Once Cade climbed aboard, Janek took the chopper clear of the Justice Department building, angling it west across New York's hazy skyline.

Cade leaned forward and activated the onboard computer, keying in a request for information on their destination. The memory banks threw text on the screen. He slumped back in the bodyform seat, staring at the monitor, but found he wasn't able to concentrate. He realized he was tired. It had been a hectic, fast-paced couple of days. There hadn't been much time for a break. Not since he and Janek had answered that first call and had burned rubber getting to the tenement building. The problems had started right there, with three murdered Justice marshals and Milt Schuberg held hostage. . . .

Cade glanced out of the chopper's canopy. The sun was setting fast now, streaking the sullen sky with multicolored bands. It was going to be a long, hot night . . . and Kansas could be even hotter.

The pulse of sound from the chopper's suppressed turbopowered engines washed over him. Cade felt his eyes closing. He activated the seat's power unit and dropped it into the sleeping position.

"I'm taking five," he said to Janek. "Spell you later."

"Fine," Janek replied. "Any time you're ready, partner."

Cade felt sleep crowding in. He didn't fight it. The last thing he heard was Janek grumbling to himself because he couldn't pick up a decent jazz station.

WHEN CADE OPENED his eyes, he realized that the helicopter was still and silent. He peered through the canopy and saw that dawn was streaking the sky. He was alone in the cabin. As the seat returned to its upright position, he noticed a message on the computer screen: "Be back shortly. Gone to arrange some transport. Janek."

Opening the hatch, Cade stepped out into the chill Kansas morning. The chopper rested on a landing pad in a corner of a small airstrip. The strip's main building and control tower stood dark and empty at this early hour. It only took Cade a minute to realize he was the only one around the place. The bite of the early-morning breeze penetrated his open jacket. Cade fished out a cigar and lit it, then zipped up his leather jacket, turning up the collar. He took a turn around the chopper, then decided he might as well sit inside where it was warmer. He climbed back into the cabin and sealed the hatch. On an impulse he picked up the handset and punched in the department's code, waiting while the radio signal was beamed up to the Justice Department's orbiting communications satellite, then down to the New York office.

"Cade," he said when the duty tech came on. "Patch me through to Braddock if he's in."

"T.J.?" Braddock's voice was as clear as if he were sitting beside Cade. "Listen good. Harrigan wasn't the only one on the payroll. Milt Schuberg got the goods on a detective in his own division. A routine bust picked the guy up with known associates of the Outfit. He decided it was in his best interest to cooperate. It looks like this mother was Brak's own personal inside man. He's been feeding Brak info for weeks. Right up to the split and beyond. Brak knows you're on his trail. He has Mid Town locked up tight. The guy who runs Mid State Freight is Brak's man. The way it's going down, he has the local cops on his payroll, as well...."

The radio fell silent. Cade tried to reconnect with New York, but the set was dead. He made a function check, running it through the computer. The screen laid it out in clear, cold text.

Someone had jammed the frequency.

"Damn!" Cade said, tossing aside the useless handset.

He reached behind him and grabbed hold of the closest combat shotgun. He checked the loads and cocked the weapon. Breaking the seal on the hatch, he climbed out of the chopper, loosening the zipper on his jacket so he could get at the Magnum. Now he didn't even feel the cold. Once he was outside, he closed the hatch and set the electro-lock. The hatch was sealed and could only be opened via a code sequence.

He moved around the chopper, scanning the area. Nothing. Except for the soft ripple of the breeze, the airstrip was silent and deserted.

Cade's ears picked up the sound of an engine. He turned in its direction and saw a slow-moving blue-and-white police cruiser rolling through the perimeter gate. The cruiser's lights hit him between the eyes, blinding him for a moment. Cade threw up a hand, turning his face away.

The cruiser kept on coming, picking up speed until it was no more than twenty feet from the chopper. As it rolled to a stop, a harsh voice crackled from its PA system:

"Put the weapon down, Cade. You're well covered. We've got your cyborg partner in here, as well. There's a gun on him. You fail to cooperate, he gets a slug through his eyepiece and that's the end of him. Your choice, mister."

The cruiser rolled to a stop. The rear doors opened and figures emerged. Even in the gray dawn light Cade recognized Janek's tall figure. The cyborg was accompanied by a burly, uniformed cop who was easily as tall. The cop had the muzzle of a powerful autopistol jammed hard against Janek's right eye.

"Your call, Cade."

Other figures emerged from the front of the cruiser, all of them aiming heavy weapons at Cade.

"Don't listen to this creep," Janek called. "I'm expendable."

Even if he'd been free and clear to take on the opposition, Cade wouldn't have put Janek at risk. He was almost relieved he didn't have to make the choice. With the hardware aimed at him, the decision was out of his hands. There was no way he could take on the kind of odds facing him. Not now. He'd have to wait for his chance.

One of the cops moved forward, his autorifle trained on Cade's chest. He reached out to take Cade's SPAS, passing it to one of his buddies. Then he frisked the Justice cop and relieved him of the Magnum. He grinned suddenly.

"Now we can relax, Cade. Welcome to Kansas," he said. Then he swung the butt of his rifle and clouted Cade across the side of the head.

The dawn exploded with brilliant light. Cade went down on his knees, feeling blood pouring across his face. The light began to fade, and darkness rolled in like a heavy tide. In the distance he heard the cop's words echoing faintly.

"Welcome to Kansas...."

And then it all slipped away.

6

Kansas

"We blew it this time," Janek said quietly.

Cade, still holding his pounding skull, eyed his cyborg partner with a less than sympathetic stare. "Not so much 'we' blew it.... From where I'm sitting 'we' translates as 'you.'"

Janek shrugged crookedly. "Okay, I can live with that. I suppose you'll want an apology."

"I'd rather have my damn Magnum."

The cop beside the driver, in the front seat of the cruiser, pointed at Cade with the rifle he was holding.

"Can't you pair quit yappin'?" he growled. "Jesus, I'll be glad when we can finish you off."

"Why didn't we do it back at the strip?" asked one of the cops sitting in the back with Cade and Janek. "Why waste time driving them all the way to town?"

"Brak wants to have words. And if the guy wants words, he gets 'em."

"He must be paying you bastards good money," Cade said with unconcealed contempt.

The cop beside Janek nodded, his face dark with anger. "Damn fuckin' right he is. He's payin' me well enough so I'll do exactly what he wants."

"Good for you," Janek said. "I'll bet you're really proud of yourself."

The cop laughed harshly. "Listen to the damn cybo preaching at me. Listen, droid, I don't give a cold kiss in hell. Take a look out there. It's a shit world, and you get one chance to make your mark. I ain't about to work my friggin' butt off cruising the streets for a lousy pension. I want my goodies now, while I can still enjoy 'em. So up your tin ass."

"That's what I like about this job, T.J. I get to meet people of such high intellect."

"One more word out of you, droid, and you get a slug right through your damn eyeball," the cop said, the muzzle of his autopistol swiveling to center on Janek. "You hear me?"

Janek nodded, letting his shoulders droop in what appeared to be acceptance of his fate.

The cop's lips formed a thin smile of triumph. He moved the muzzle back toward Cade.

Janek sat upright, his right hand springing forward, fingers clamping over the cop's wrist. The cyborg twisted sharply. The cop's high screech of pain drowned the sound of his wrist bones snapping. His fingers slackened their grip on the gun butt, and it dropped. Janek caught it with his left hand, slashing it up and around. The hard metal cracked against the cop's lower jaw. Skin burst, and blood spurted as the cop fell away.

The moment Janek moved, Cade erupted. His right elbow smashed into the throat of the cop at his side. The guy began to choke, clutching his damaged throat. Cade reached around and caught hold of the cop's hair. He dragged the moaning guy close to him, then shoved his face down against his own rising knee. Bone cracked, and the guy's nose began to blossom red.

The cop in the front passenger seat made a grab for the rifle resting between his knees. The cyborg didn't hesitate. He angled the autopistol across the back of the seat and triggered a single shot into the back of the renegade cop's skull. The guy was slammed forward, a bloody spray tinting the windshield.

The driver stepped on the brake, sending the cruiser in a sideways slide across the road. Fighting the wheel with one hand, he snatched his handgun with the other. Twisting in his seat, he opened fire, slugs shattering the rear window of the cruiser

Cade punched the door handle on his side. When the door sprang open, he shoved out the groaning cop he'd hit, following him. The cop hit the pavement with Cade on top. The Justice cop rolled clear, lurching to his feet, and saw Janek leaping from the opposite side of the cruiser just before it picked up speed again. The powerful vehicle roared along the road for a distance, then turned, burning rubber as the driver hauled the wheel around.

"Go!" Cade yelled, shoving Janek across the pavement.

They cleared the road, diving headlong into the dusty brush edging it, then regained their feet and ran.

Behind them the cruiser braked noisily, engine roaring as the driver slammed it into reverse, then forward again. The heavy cruiser sent up clouds of acrid dust as it slithered across the bumpy terrain.

"Where the hell we going?" Cade asked as he paced alongside Janek.

"That, Thomas, is a stupid question at this moment in time," the cyborg replied.

"Only because you haven't got an answer!" Cade yelled.

It was academic. They were running for their lives across a stretch of dusty Kansas flatland. There was no visible cover in sight, nothing but the eroded plain with its miles and miles of emptiness.

The sound of the cruiser grew louder behind them, rising to a high wail. Without warning, the engine faltered and coughed.

Cade turned and saw the vehicle had got itself bogged down in a patch of soft earth. Great clouds of dust billowed from under the rear wheels.

"I don't believe it," he breathed.

Janek stood beside him, watching the cruiser closely.

Peering through the dust still drifting around the stalled cruiser, Janek spotted the driver moving inside the vehicle. "Damn!" Janek snapped. "He's using his radio to call for backup."

The cyborg's keen vision enabled him to focus on distant objects and bring them into close relief.

Janek raised the handgun and laid a fast trio of shots through the windshield. He was rewarded by the sight of the driver flopping against the seat's backrest, blood

streaming down his face from the wound in his forehead.

Circling the vehicle, Janek approached it from the
rear, autopistol held before him.

Making the most of the moment, Cade crouched
beside the cop he'd bundled out of the cruiser. The guy
was stretched out across the road, groaning softly. He
didn't offer any resistance when Cade took his holstered autopistol. Cutting around the rear of the
cruiser, Cade covered Janek as the cyborg moved in.

"Okay, T.J., we're clear," Janek said, straightening
up.

"Anything in there?" he asked Janek.

The cyborg shook his head.

"You reckon he got through to whoever he was calling?"

"Could be," Janek said. He scanned the area. "We
could be getting visitors any time, Thomas. It might be
wise to get the hell away from here."

Cade took a slow look around. "Any more bright
suggestions?"

"No, but I think we should still move. Maybe we can
find a phone. We need to call Braddock, let him know
what we've found here. Maybe he can get the area
Justice Department to send some backup."

Cade opened the cruiser's trunk and retrieved their
weapons, stowed there after their captors had disarmed them. He passed Janek his handgun, then
strapped on his Magnum. As an afterthought Cade
scooped up the autorifle from the front of the cruiser,
and rummaged for a couple of spare magazines.

"Come on, hotshot, let's move out."

They tramped across the dusty flatland, anxious to put some distance between themselves and the stalled cruiser.

Daylight was flooding the land now. The rising sun threw bright shafts of light over the landscape, leaving Cade and Janek exposed.

"T.J., are you still blaming me for what happened?" Janek asked out of the blue. He had been thinking about the matter. Now, he decided, was the time to bring it into the open.

Cade looked across at the cyborg. He could tell from Janek's expression that his partner was in his serious mode. For all his developing human tendencies, Janek still relied on his programmed responses to certain situations. Like now. He felt responsible for the turn of events and would relentlessly badger Cade about them until he got a satisfactory answer.

"No sweat, partner," Cade said. "The situation got a little out of hand is all. But we're back on stream, so why all the fuss?"

"It could have got you killed. That isn't supposed to happen when I'm around."

"I'm fine, Janek. The only thing worrying me is how we get out of this."

"Thomas, you're avoiding the question," Janek persisted.

Cade stopped dead in his tracks. "Okay," he exploded. "That's it. I try to let you off the hook easy. But no, you have to go on about it. Acting like some two-bit martyr. 'Sorry, T.J. I've been a bad partner, T.J., tell me off so I can rest easy, T.J.' Well, yeah, you fucked up, pal. Real good. Lined the pair of us up like beer cans on a fence just waiting to be shot down. Next time tell me when you decide to go off on your own. At least do that so I can expect you to come back with the bad guys and not get caught with my pants down. Okay?''

Janek peered at him silently. After a minute he shook his head, face solemn. "You're not just saying that, are you, Thomas?"

Cade didn't trust himself to speak. He simply carried on walking, checking the way ahead. He heard Janek coming up behind him, and a moment later the cybo fell in step beside him.

"I think I may have broken that code," he stated, the previous confrontation already forgotten.

"Took your time," Cade said. "You slowing down?"

"Well, I've had other things on my mind."

"Let's hear what you've got."

"I'm starting to make sense out of all those figures and numbers. I believe what we have is a list of names, bank accounts, their relevant numbers and locations."

"How soon before you get it all clear?"

"Very soon," Janek said confidently. "When I get a quiet minute, I'll be able to transcribe it."

The air was suddenly filled with the pulsing sound of an air cruiser. Someone was pushing the craft to its limit. As Cade turned, glancing skyward, the cruiser's shadow fell over the Justice cops.

The air cruiser was a private craft, unmarked. It was painted a dull ocher red with a silver stripe. It overshot, passing no more than ten feet from them, then banked steeply, starting to come around in a tight curve.

Cade saw the oil-streaked underside clearly. He made out the complex pattern of ducting tubes running from the turbine engine's hover cowl. Then the sleek cruiser cleared them, heat waves shimmering from its exhausts. He was able to see the plasglass canopy and the blurred shapes of three passengers.

"Trust you to mention a quiet minute," Cade said, unlimbering the autorifle.

He searched the area for cover. There was only uneven, dusty flatland with little cover to offer except the odd clump of thicket.

Leveling off, the air cruiser dropped almost to ground level. It streaked in at Cade and Janek, trailing a wide spume of dust. The pilot swung the craft around in a sudden broadside, kicking in the hover power to bring the craft to a swaying midair stop. The rear portion of the canopy slid open with a hiss of air pistons. One of the passengers in the rear swung a heavy black autoweapon through the opening. The wide muzzle flamed, sending a stream of large-caliber slugs at Cade and Janek.

Cade had moved the moment the canopy opened, expecting the worst. He felt the earth tremble underfoot as the slugs pounded the ground. Dirt and stones peppered the back of his legs as he took a long, desperate leap. He hit the ground hard, gasping as his breath was slammed from his lungs, but he ignored the momentary paralysis of his breathing function and kept rolling, the autorifle tucked in tight against his chest.

He stopped by a tough clump of thicket. Cade's head came up. Spitting dust, he blinked away from the sweat stinging his eyes and glanced back at the cruiser. It was still hovering. The gunner had altered his aim. He was sending burst after burst at Janek's weaving figure. The cyborg was leading the gunner through an erratic course, causing him to constantly retrack.

"That crazy droid," Cade muttered, rising to his feet. He shouldered the autorifle, locking the weapon's laser sight on the distant gunner. Cade activated the autoranger, his finger caressing the pretrigger. He felt the trigger release, activating the secondary trigger. All that was needed was the lightest touch. Cade breathed in and held, then stroked the cold curve of metal. He felt the rifle kick back gently, the powerful blast absorbed by the recoil block.

The impact threw the gunner across the cruiser's compartment. For a moment the guy hung on the rim of the open canopy, then fell with a scared yell.

Twenty feet below, his body raised a cloud of dust as it crashed to the ground. He lay in a messy sprawl, legs and arms twitching.

Cade ran forward, aiming the rifle again. He fired at the cruiser's power plant. The slugs penetrated the lower deck plates, and smoke began to creep from the holes. A black finger of hot oil fluttered from a punctured pipe. The cruiser began to sink as the operator tried to gain some forward motion. But the craft's hover capabilities were fading rapidly. It sank quickly, smoke billowing from the rear. The cruiser dropped the final few feet and hit the ground with a heavy crash.

Approaching from the opposite side, Janek saw an armed figure kick aside the shattered canopy and scramble over the cruiser's side. The guy spotted Janek as he touched the ground. With an angry yell he swung up a squat handgun and pumped a stream of shots at the cyborg.

Janek felt something tug at his left arm. In response, he leveled his rifle, planting two slugs directly over the guy's heart. The shots pinned the guy to the side of the crippled cruiser. He looked down at the twin holes in his chest, seemingly fascinated by the sight of his own blood pumping from the ragged wounds. He released his gun, and it dropped to the ground. Then he slumped facedown in the blood-spattered dust.

Janek reached the downed cruiser moments ahead of Cade. They both covered the cruiser's operator before realizing the guy, slumped over the controls, posed no threat. When Janek reached out to touch him, he slid sideways, his head flopping loosely, eyes staring in the empty glare of death.

"They don't give up easy," Cade said softly. "And these won't be the last."

"It's their choice," Janek said, and even Cade caught the cold edge to his words.

Janek hauled the dead operator out of the cruiser, leaned into the compartment and scanned it thoroughly.

"You looking for anything in particular?" Cade asked.

"No, but it won't do to pass anything over, T.J."

Janek straightened up, smirking self-righteously.

"Found something?"

"Only the registration ticket. Confirms this cruiser belongs to Mid State Freight."

Kneeling beside the guy he'd shot, Janek went through the dead man's pockets. He came up with a billfold that held a driver's license, money and credit cards, among other things.

"Eddie Franco," Janek read. "I know that name from police records. He's a known felon from the East Side. Generally hired himself out to the highest bidder. I'd say we've got one of Brak's running mates here, T.J."

Cade picked up Franco's stubby autopistol and examined it. "This is one of those new Swiss handguns. The one the department tested out a few months back. The damn things aren't supposed to be in the country yet."

Janek stood, taking the gun and running his expert eye over it. "Fine piece of weaponry," he observed. "So let's evaluate our position. Right now we have enough to connect this local bunch with Brak. A link with Mid State. A New York felon carrying an illegal weapon. I'd say we've got more than enough to give Mid State a shakedown."

"God, I hate it when you talk like a robot," Cade said. "All that stuff you've been quoting is fine, but it does jack shit for our position. Janek, we're in the middle of nowhere. High and dry and more than likely to get our lights punched any minute. We're in great shape, pal."

Janek considered his partner's words. "Put that way, Thomas, we are caught between a rock and a hard place." Then the cyborg brightened considerably. "But at least we have company!"

Cade picked up the soft footsteps behind him and turned.

He found himself face-to-face with a half-dozen silent, hostile-looking Mutants.

7

It had been a long time since Cade had been face-to-face with a Mutant. He eyed them with caution, but remained fairly impassive himself. He had no reason to show any aggression for the moment. The main problem with Mutants was their instability; they changed mood from passive gentleness to terrifying violence quickly and without warning. He'd seen it happen, and recalled the memory as he confronted the group before him now.

They were clad in the universal dress of Mutants nationwide, an odd blend of handmade and manufactured garments. Due to the often extreme genetic disfigurement that afflicted most Mutants, their clothing afforded them comfort, as well as concealment. The fabric was heavy, designed more for this kind of terrain than city dwelling.

Few Mutants ventured near large cities, where much ignorance and hostility were directed at them. As with most prejudices it was misguided and founded on superstition. After being the victims of raw violence, the Mutants realized they were safer with their own kind. They stayed in the wastelands, creating their own settlements far away from the megacities.

"What happened here?" one of the Mutants asked, peering at the dead men and the downed cruiser.

He was a big man, broad, with heavy shoulders and long, muscular arms. His large hands each had a thumb and three fingers. He watched Cade closely, his wide-set eyes unblinking in his angular, big-boned face. The flesh, brown and weathered, was oddly grained and textured like a reptile's.

Cade pulled his badge and held it up for them all to see.

"T. J. Cade," he announced. "Justice marshal. He's my partner, Marshal Janek."

"You're not from here," the Mutant said sharply.

"New York," Janek said. "Trailing a gang of drug traffickers. They have a local connection and didn't take to us interfering."

The Mutant eased by Cade and stood in front of Janek. He looked the cyborg up and down, head rocking from side to side, deep sounds rising in his throat. "Different," he decided. "This one's different."

A second Mutant shuffled forward with an awkward gait, favoring a twisted right leg. One side of his lean, pale white flesh was marred by a thick growth of horny flesh that formed a half mask from hairline to throat. He stared at Janek with his single eye.

"Yeah," he said almost immediately. His voice had a clipped, birdlike tone. "He ain't a real one. He's a cybo. A fuckin' freak."

He began to laugh, a shrill warble of sound that burst from his tight, thin mouth.

The first Mutant peered at Janek. "He right, Marshal? You a cybo? A freak?"

Janek nodded.

"Hah! Lec always knows. He can sniff a cybo a day away."

"Interesting," Janek observed. "How does he do it?"

The Mutant shrugged. "Don' know. Even Lec couldn't tell you, but he still can do it."

Lec was still laughing, swinging around on his awkward limbs to wave his arms at his companions. "How do I do it? Only Lec knows and he ain't tellin'."

"I hate to break up the party," Cade said tautly.

The first Mutant swung around on him. "You not in New York now, Cade. This is *our* territory. That badge you carry don't mean nothin' out here. We could kill you, and no one would ever find your bones."

"Yeah," Lec crowed. "We *eat* your bones."

"Bullshit is all you'll eat," Cade warned. The authority in his words silenced them all—even Lec. "I don't want trouble with you people. Just let me get on with my job, and you can go your own way."

"Maybe we'll kill you just for the hell of it," the big Mutant said.

"You got a name?" Cade asked.

"I'm Tragg, the Mutant said. "Why'd you want to know?"

"It's easier dealing with a man when you know his name," Janek said hastily, stepping in front of Cade. "Let's keep this friendly. Maybe you can help us."

Tragg glanced across at the cyborg. "You mean that?"

"Sure."

"Hey, Tragg, you see who these shag-asses are?" a skeletal Mutant said. He was tall and pale, with red eyes that seemed to glow even in the daylight. His thin hair, almost white, hung in tangled strands down his hunched spine.

Tragg crossed to check out the dead men. He muttered something, turning back to fix Cade with a hard stare. "These mothers were after you," he said. "We saw them chasin' you."

"So?"

Tragg gave a crooked smile. "We got more in common than you realize, Cade. You know who they are?"

"Do you?"

"Yeah. Except for that one," Tragg said, indicating the New York perp. "He's a stranger. The others are Dekker's boys. From Mid State."

Lec, leaning over one of the dead men, spit on the body. "Better dead than hunting us," he said bitterly.

"Doesn't sound like you're big fans," Cade suggested.

"You ever been in Mid Town?" Tragg asked.

Cade grinned. "We kind of got diverted."

Tragg gave a roar of laughter. "Diverted! You call bein' hunted a diversion?"

"A temporary delay in our schedule," Janek said stiffly.

"Dekker won't see it like that," Tragg stated. "He's a mean one, Cade. Finding his boys dead is only going to make him meaner."

"If this Dekker is involved with the people we're after, he's already on his way out," Cade said.

"You get rid of Dekker, you get my vote," Lec said.

"He caused you people trouble?"

Tragg nodded. "We only go to town odd times. Try not to bother anyone. But it's a mean place. We only go there because of the freight yards. It's a bad place sometimes. Dekker is the boss. He runs Mid State. Biggest outfit there. Anyone else wants to operate, they go to Dekker and he takes a cut. He has a hand in every business going. And the local law is his."

"We already met them," Janek said.

"You said you were after drug traffickers? Word is that Dekker does some haulin' for an outfit back east." Tragg jerked a thumb at the dead New York perp. "This one of them?"

Cade nodded. "There's been a fallout in the organization. One of the top guys has decided to get rid of his partners and run the whole thing himself. We followed him from N.Y. Figured he'd stop here to make a new deal with the local handler. Looks like he already did."

"Bastards," Tragg breathed angrily. "They have a game in town when some of our people go there. Grab a couple and shoot them full of those crystals they peddle. Has a bad effect on us, Cade. Hurts us more than normal people. The dreams can kill and usually do. If we don't die, we end up with scrambled brains."

"Tragg, we need to get into Dekker's place. You want his operation closed down? Help us get inside. Can you do it?"

Lec chuckled. "Can Lec smell out a cybo?"

"We can get you in."

Cade caught Janek's eye. "Collect all the hardware you can," he said. "I want to hit Dekker fast and hard. Take his operation down to the foundations."

"How long will it take to reach Mid Town?"

"On foot a long time," Tragg said. "But we got transport."

Lec, following Janek to pick up the weapons, said, "Hey, cybo, you ever ride a horse?"

"T.J., I don't think I'm going to like this."

"Think about it while we move out. I don't want to be surprised twice in one day."

Tragg gestured in the general direction of the west. "We have a place out there," he said. "Near the Chemlands. It's about five miles. There's food and the horses."

The Mutants led the Justice cops to a small settlement hidden in a natural basin on the edge of the local Chemlands. The area beyond the settlement took on a distinct change. The terrain was darker, the landscape dotted with choking tracts of heavy vegetation and stunted trees. Mutations had been created in the aftermath of the missile strikes of the U.S.–Islamic Federation war. The terrible spillages from the warheads had germinated and developed strange new strains of plant and wildlife. And the human animal hadn't escaped. Humanlike Mutants roved the Outlands, shunning society.

A low-lying mist hung over the area, rolling slowly in and out of the vegetation. The mist emanated from the numerous biopits that frothed and bubbled like festering scabs on the land, spewing out a deadly rain of toxic waste.

Tragg explained that the Chemlands lay in the shape of a great crescent, forming a barrier between the settlement and Mid Town. No one from town would venture near the Chemlands because so much was still unknown about the place. Staying away was the wise and accepted thing to do. The Chemlands offered a sanctuary for Tragg and his kind, a place where they could hide in desperate moments, their altered forms able to survive the poisonous mists.

Cade could detect the fetid stench that wafted across the dusty plain between the settlement and the Chemlands. He knew the stink well and hated it. During his time with the Marines, he'd had to work around the Chemlands. He hadn't liked it then and didn't like it now.

"You don' like the biopits," Lec said. It wasn't a question. The Mutant could sense Cade's feelings and turn them into words. "You have bad memories?"

"Something like that," Cade said, not wanting to elaborate.

Lec scuttled to Janek's side. He had developed some kind of rapport with the cyborg, possibly because he thought of him as a freak. "Hey, you'll like the horses," he said.

"You think so?" Janek was unconvinced. His understanding of horses was that they were powerful, unreliable creatures that had a habit of throwing their riders.

"On a horse I'm as good as any man," Lec stated, grinning. "My legs don't matter then. The horse has four, enough for both of us."

Twice during the journey to the settlement they spotted helicopters making long, wide sweeps of the area. Janek's long-range vision enabled him to pick out the aircrafts' markings as belonging to the Mid Town police. The Mutants, used to avoiding detection, were able to guide the Justice cops into hiding. After the second chopper made its appearance, they saw no more.

They walked through the settlement. It was little more than a collection of ramshackle huts constructed from scrap timber and aluminum sheets, bonded together with mud. The Mutants were transient, never staying too long in one spot. Wherever possible they grew their own food and hunted game if there was any about. Often they had to steal to eat. In some areas they were able to pick up laboring jobs. It was a bleak existence, but the Mutants bore it in stoic silence, aware that they had no choice. They were small in number, their clout nonexistent, so they made the best of their lives.

In the early years, as the Mutant population developed, there had been many suicides. Many of them had been unable to handle what had happened to them. Ostracized by society, blamed for something that wasn't their fault, some had collapsed under the unbearable pressure, and taken the only way out they could find. Others accepted the government offers of resettlement on the space colonies, where society was developing in a different way and mutations were accepted. This solved part of the problem. But there were thousands of Mutants who had no desire to leave the mother planet, preferring to stay despite the restrictions.

A great many Mutants were intelligent and put that quality to good use. Though the settlements were primitive in most respects, the Mutants used their ingenuity to develop forms of power and provide at least the basics of life. As Cade wandered through Tragg's settlement, he saw solar power being used for cooking and lighting, even powering a small generator that operated a battered but serviceable TV set.

"I know what you were going to say," Tragg said bluntly as Cade turned to him. "If we're so capable, why don't we improve our lives?"

Cade smiled ruefully. "Pretty close."

"Why should we? Look what too much technology brought us, Cade."

The horses were penned in a corral constructed from long lengths of timber. The animals were rangy, bright eyed and eager to meet the newcomers.

"Better than a car," Tragg said. "They feed off the land and they'll take us anywhere we want to go."

"I'm beginning to wonder if you haven't got the best end of the deal, Tragg," Cade said.

"But not for you? A city boy to the last."

They sat around a log fire and ate. Cade silently studied the grouped Mutants, women and children alike, and realized after a while that he and Janek were the outsiders here. The Mutants were living their lives as they always had while the Justice cops brought memories of another culture, another world.

Tragg drew Cade and Janek aside after the meal. He used a sharpened stick to sketch a layout of Mid Town for them in the dirt.

"Mid State is here, on the north edge of town. They have the best site. Railroad runs right on by the freight yard, so Mid State can load or unload easily. Loading bays feed right up to the railroad tracks here and here. On the other side of the warehouses the same applies for the road rigs. Offices are built over the storage sheds. They even have sleeping and eating accommodation for the teams who drive the rigs."

"Security?" Janek asked.

"Run by the local law force. Owned by Mid State. Police chief is called Thornton. He's bad, Cade. A really bad apple. He shouldn't be running a jail—he should be in it. Thornton's a big guy with short-cropped red hair."

"The police who picked us up at the airstrip were Mid Town," Janek said. "So we know Thornton is already in Brak's pocket. What we can't be sure of yet is how the cards are going to fall. We could have so many of the Outfit's people staying loyal to the old regime and some moving over to Brak. And he may be hiring his own new people, as well."

"Don't rule out the Outfit sending in reinforcements. Shultz and Lorenzo aren't going to let Brak get away without a fight," Cade said.

"Sounds to me like one hell of a mess," Tragg said.

"All in a day's work," Cade said.

"When do you want to move in?" Tragg asked.

"I'd like to choose my time," Cade replied. "But I don't have that luxury. Brak's on the move, setting up his operation as he goes. I have to take my shots the minute I see them. So we can move any time you're ready."

AN HOUR LATER they were riding across the dusty Kansas plain, following an unmarked trail that would bring them in on the far side of Mid Town from behind a range of low hills.

Tragg was in the lead, Lec bringing up the tail end. In between were Cade and Janek.

The horses needed little guidance. They knew the way and took it at their own pace. Cade sat on his homemade saddle with self-conscious unease. He felt like a character out of an old Western. After a half hour of the swaying ride he decided John Wayne was welcome to it. The dust, the heat and the constant swarm of flies convinced him that riding in a cruiser was a damn sight more comfortable.

As far as Janek was concerned, the horse as a means of transport was definitely something out of a nightmare. He found nothing to praise—but a lot to criticize. He mastered the art of sitting in the saddle and controlling the horse with no trouble. After that the whole experience nose-dived. The cyborg, registering the horse's rocking movements, figured the human race had to be crazy to fall in love with such a mode of transport—uncomfortable, slow and boring.

He reviewed the code numbers from the traffickers' computers. The sequence of numbers and figures, constantly being analyzed deep in the recesses of his electronic brain, were beginning to make sense. At this stage they were no more than spaghetti. Scanning

THE GOLD EAGLE TEAM IS ON THE MOVE AGAIN WITH FOUR NEW MINISERIES IN 1993 PROVIDING YOU WITH THE BEST IN ACTION ADVENTURE!

Omega Force is the last—and deadliest—option

PATRICK F. ROGERS

OMEGA

WAR MACHINE

Gold Eagle brings another fast-paced miniseries to the action adventure front—**OMEGA**—featuring a special antiterrorist strike force composed of the best commandos and equipment the military has to offer.

WAR MACH!NE: Book #1 of this paramilitary miniseries will be available in February 1993. Look for Books #2 and #3 in June and October. (224 pages, $3.50 each)

The Peacekeepers are ready—the toughest grunts on the planet

WARKEEP 2030

KILLING FIELDS
Michael Kasner

Introducing the follow-up miniseries to the popular **WARKEEP 2030** title published in November 1992.

This miniseries tracks the Peacekeepers, an elite military force that tries to impose peace in the troubled 21st century. Look for Book 1: **KILLING FIELDS** in March. Books #2 and #3 continue in July and November. (224 pages, $3.50 each)

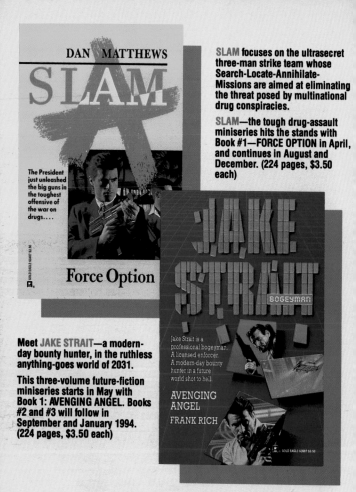

SLAM focuses on the ultrasecret three-man strike team whose Search-Locate-Annihilate-Missions are aimed at eliminating the threat posed by multinational drug conspiracies.

SLAM—the tough drug-assault miniseries hits the stands with Book #1—FORCE OPTION in April, and continues in August and December. (224 pages, $3.50 each)

DAN MATTHEWS

SLAM

The President just unleashed the big guns in the toughest offensive of the war on drugs....

Force Option

JAKE STRAIT BOGEYMAN

Jake Strait is a professional bogeyman. A licensed enforcer. A modern-day bounty hunter in a future world shot to hell.

AVENGING ANGEL

FRANK RICH

Meet **JAKE STRAIT**—a modern-day bounty hunter, in the ruthless anything-goes world of 2031.

This three-volume future-fiction miniseries starts in May with Book 1: AVENGING ANGEL. Books #2 and #3 will follow in September and January 1994. (224 pages, $3.50 each)

Make sure you're part of the action—
JOIN THE GOLD EAGLE TEAM WITH MORE EXPLOSIVE TITLES COMING YOUR WAY IN 1993!

Available at your favorite retail stores.

GES93
PRINTED IN CANADA

them, Janek was able to translate them into some kind of order. He pushed them back through the circuits, tidying up the haphazard jumble, seeking the key that would cause them to fall into place. The permutations were endless and needed constant shuffling. Janek's sophisticated brain was able to do this on an endless cycle, sifting and storing each new combination, searching, rejecting.

Then it came. The sequences unfurled, the numbers and figures scrolling into recognizable formations. Janek double-checked them, then locked the result in his frontal memory. He allowed himself a moment of congratulation, smiling as he pushed his horse alongside Cade's.

"Want to hear something interesting?"

Cade glanced at him sourly. His face was streaked with sweat and dust, and he had never looked less ready to receive information.

"I hope this isn't a lecture on the right way to sit on a damn horse."

"Not as much fun." Janek grinned. "But you'll like it."

"Don't hold your breath."

Janek resisted mentioning that he couldn't hold his breath anyway. "I've decoded the info we took from the computer "

8

Mid Town's central position made it the major distribution point for the nation's freight. Tragg's description of the place had been exact. The town itself was no more than a service area that offered everything required to keep the sprawling maze of freight yards and warehouses operating twenty-four hours a day.

The town was a noisy, neon-lit area comprised of diners and hotels, stores and a red-light district that catered to any sexual desire and deviation imaginable. Tragg had said that it was possible to buy anything you wanted in Mid Town. From the brief glimpse of the place as they led the horses along the outskirts, Cade was inclined to agree. Mid Town had the feel and sound of a wide-open frontier settlement, where the whims of the population were granted in order to keep the business side moving.

They arrived in late afternoon. Now Tragg was guiding them to the Mid State Freight yards. Both Tragg and Lec had wanted to join the Justice cops on their assault, but Cade had advised against it.

"I'm grateful for the help, Tragg, but I don't want you involved in any hostilities. If you and Lec are spotted, it's going to make it hard on your people.

Right now you have enough problems. No point adding to them."

Tragg didn't like the advice but he acknowledged Cade's reasoning.

"He talks sense, Tragg," Lec said. "Kicking ass is okay, but these bastards could hit us later when we don't have anyone around to hold 'em off. We got women and kids to think about."

"Yeah, yeah, I know."

Lec patted Janek's shoulder. "These two will leave Dekker and his bunch something to think about. Right, Janek?"

"You don't have to worry about that," the cyborg said.

Concealed behind stacks of timber, they studied the layout of the vast freight yard. Beyond the yards, thronged with powerful long-distance semitrailers being loaded and unloaded, stood the warehouses with the operations center on top.

"T.J., on the roof," Janek said. "Couple of choppers. One of them has New York registration."

Cade could see the helicopters but could not read any numbers. Janek's optical system, with its powerful magnification, allowed him to see far beyond the range of human vision.

"We could be in luck, partner," Cade said. "Could be Brak is still in town. Let's roll before he decides to move on."

"You sure you don't want us to stay around?" Tragg asked again.

"Thanks, Tragg, but no. You and Lec get back to your people."

Tragg grasped Cade's hand with his three-fingered hand. "You're not a bad mother, Cade. Maybe no Mutant, but you're okay."

"The freak ain't bad, either." Lec grinned amiably, raising a hand in farewell.

Shouldering their weapons, Cade and Janek cut across the rail tracks toward the Mid State Freight yard.

Following the rows of freight cars standing idle on the spur line, they moved closer to the yard. Crouched in the shadows beneath a white refrigerated car, they decided on their final approach.

"Rear-entrance strategy," Janek suggested. "We go in any other way, we'll attract too much attention."

Cade scanned the area. He nodded agreement. There were too many people around to allow frontal entry. Then there were the innocent workers. He didn't want to put lives at risk if things became hostile. It added another dimension to the game.

"How about the fire escape?" Cade suggested, indicating the metal structure on the end of the building. It ran from ground to roof, with access doors on each floor.

"It's all we've got," the cyborg said. He focused in on the fire escape and checked it carefully. "There's an armed guy watching the base," he said. "Probably more on the roof. Don't forget they do know we're still alive and kicking."

"As far as they know, we're still out there, wandering around, looking for a ride."

"Maybe. If I was running the operation, I'd expect the worst."

Cade ran a quick check on his powerful SMG. The weapon had a full magazine, and Cade had two more inside his jacket.

"Okay, Mr. Cautious, shall we do it?"

Janek unlimbered his own weapon, snapping back the bolt. "Ready when you are."

They broke cover, crossing an open stretch of ground that brought them behind a small building housing an oil store. Empty steel drums stacked in untidy piles provided the cover they needed while they checked the way ahead. The noise from the busy freight yard drowned any noise they might make. Dust thrown up from the constant stream of vehicles cast a drifting mist into the air that mingled with the diesel fumes pumped from the tractor units.

"Correction," Janek said. "Two men guarding the base of the fire escape. Both armed."

"I want them taken out without any noise," Cade said.

"The way they're lounging around, that shouldn't be too hard."

Cade watched the armed guards patiently. When one offered his partner a cigarette and the pair got involved in lighting up, he told Janek, "Go."

Cade slipped around the oil drum stack, watching the guards, his weapon held across his chest. At first Janek was close behind, but then he increased his power level and moved into the lead.

The guards, sensing sound and movement, turned, faces registering alarm as they saw the Justice cops. They made futile grabs for the autoweapons slung from their shoulders.

Janek caught the first guy, swinging a powerful arm around his neck and sweeping him off his feet in a rush. The guy uttered a single, startled cry as his head was slammed against the wall. He slumped to the ground without another sound. Kneeling beside him, Janek pulled a pair of plastic cuffs from a pocket and quickly secured the guard's hands behind his back.

Cade's man managed to free his weapon and slip a finger across the trigger. Then Cade's SMG clouted him across the jaw. The guy grunted, feeling the hot gush of blood spill over his shirt. Cade hit him again, hard in the belly, doubling the guy over, and followed through with a knee into the guy's jaw as he toppled. Cuffing him, Cade relieved him of the compact walk-ie-talkie clipped to his belt.

Jerking his thumb toward the fire escape, Cade snatched up his SMG and followed close on Janek's heels. The cybo climbed the metal stairs fast, reaching the top well before his human partner. By the time Cade reached him, the cyborg had pinpointed the pair of armed guards on the flat roof.

Peering over the parapet, Cade checked out the two choppers resting on the painted landing pad. The one bearing New York registration numbers stood beside a powerful pursuit model painted blue and white, with the legend Mid Town Police Department on its side.

"We could be getting lucky," Cade said. "Looks as if the whole damn gang is home."

"I'll believe it when I see it," Janek muttered.

"Let's get this party on the road."

Cade crept silently toward the closer guard. The guy had barely turned his back when Cade reached him.

Snaking an arm over the guard's shoulder, Cade locked his forearm over his opponent's windpipe, yanking back hard. Choking, the guard reached up to claw at Cade's arm, forgetting about the autoweapon dangling from his shoulder. The more he struggled the tighter Cade's arm locked around his throat. Heaving back, the Justice cop lifted the man off his feet. Panic began to set in as the guard's entire body weight dragged against the arm at his throat. He thrashed about, his choking turning into a harsh cough.

Janek turned his full attention to the other guard. This guy was some twelve feet away, facing them. As he noticed Cade, the second guard made a grab for his autoweapon. Janek vaulted the parapet, his feet digging in as he hit the roof. The cyborg's ability to accelerate quickly became self-evident as he powered across the roof, covering the distance in a time no human could have contemplated.

The guard, still pulling up his weapon, saw little more than a swift moving shape hurtling in his direction. He had no time to retaliate or even move aside. Janek's powerful shoulder smashed into the guard's chest and pushed him across the roof in a helpless tangle.

Dazed and gasping for breath, the guard tried to push Janek aside as the cyborg bent over him. He felt himself in the grip of powerful hands. Janek hauled the man to his feet, using one hand to rip the autoweapon from his shoulder. Janek searched under the guard's jacket and located a handgun, which he pulled from its holster and tossed aside. Without a word the cyborg crossed to the parapet, raised the guard and swung him over the edge, letting his legs dangle in space.

"Question time," the cybo said coldly. "I ask, you answer, and it had better be the right one."

"Jesus Christ!" the guard croaked, still trying to regain his breath. "You crazy or something?"

"I said I'll ask—you just answer. Or I'll drop you."

The guard glanced down between his swaying feet, not liking what he saw. His scared eyes flicked back to Janek's impassive features. "What?" he pleaded.

"Dekker's office?"

The guard waved an arm in the direction of the roof's access door. "Through the door. Bottom of the stairs and along the passage. Double doors at the end. Dekker's office."

Janek held the man's gaze, letting long seconds slip by.

"It's the truth, man," the guard whined. He was really getting scared now.

Janek let his arm sag a fraction, just to emphasize his point. "You won't be going anywhere, so it better be the truth."

He pulled the guard back over the parapet, spun the trembling guy around and cuffed his wrists and ankles. "Sit down and stay there," Janek said, seeing Cade approach.

He turned to his partner. "Follow me," Janek said breezily as Cade rejoined him.

They reached the door and slipped down the stairs. At the bottom a passage stretched away from them. The walls and ceiling were tastefully decorated, accented by concealed lighting and expensive floor covering. The double doors at the far end were protected by a gleaming security droid.

"Looks like we need some ethnic input here, bro," Cade said dryly.

"The human intellect at its basest," Janek observed. "But I'll bail you out for old times' sake."

The cyborg handed Cade his SMG as he stepped off the stairs and along the passage.

Registering Janek's approach, the sec-droid activated itself and stepped forward, raising a massive titanium steel hand.

"I don't know you," the droid said, its voice flat and mechanical. Janek recognized the model; it was ten years old and primitive by his standards. The sec-droid had a limited-mode performance range.

Janek took out his badge and held it up. The droid's eyes flickered as it scanned the bar code.

"Marshal Janek, may I help you?" Programmed to respect authority, the droid was incapable of resisting Janek's presence.

"I need you to submit to a Code-14 inspection," Janek said evenly.

The droid stepped forward, turning slightly, accessing a small panel in its side. This allowed official inspection of its program system by authorized personnel. The Code-14 legislation had been introduced to prevent anyone altering android programming for illegal purposes. Janek needed access for a different reason. He reached into the cavity, bypassing the normal check terminals, and keyed in an override sequence that shut off the droid's power. The steel droid became inanimate.

Janek waved Cade to join him, taking back his weapons.

"That was neat," Cade said, indicating the droid.

Janek inclined his head. "It was nothing," he said coyly.

"Shall we dance, partner?" Cade said, raising one booted foot and slamming it against the doors.

The doors flew open with a crash.

"Justice Department, folks," Cade announced as he went into Dekker's plush office. "Nobody moves—nobody gets hurt."

9

Cade followed his warning with decisive action, aware that any hesitation would lose him his advantage. He moved into the spacious office, with its panoramic window and expensive furniture, the SMG covering the tight group of men clustered around a computer console.

"I want to see everybody's hands! Now! No sneaky moves or this goes off."

"His doesn't, mine will," Janek added, swinging the doors shut and standing with his back to them.

"Cade! You stupid bastard!" Chief Thornton yelled angrily. There was no mistaking his identity. The big man's cropped red hair and dark uniform stood out clearly. "You're a fuckin' idiot if you think you can bust into my town and get away with it."

"Sounds like another John Wayne fan," Janek murmured quietly so only Cade could hear. "He'll want a noon showdown next."

"What's that droid sayin'?" Thornton raged. His wide face was fast turning as red as his hair. "Jesus, I hate mouthy droids."

"Best not to start him off, then," Cade advised.

He was checking out the group as he spoke.

Just behind Thornton, the local police chief, Loren Brak was eyeing Cade with a surly expression. Lean and sleek, his wiry frame clad in expensive designer clothes, he had the look of a barely-tamed wild animal. His eyes were bright with reckless anger. Cade's sudden appearance was threatening his grand plan. Brak's scheme was beginning to crumble, and he had too much invested in it to allow that to happen. Cade decided he was going to have to keep a close eye on the man.

Dekker, identified by a tag on his tan work shirt, was holding himself in check with obvious difficulty. Anger flared in his narrow eyes. Cade figured Dekker would be a dangerous man if let loose. A true believer in the power of brute force.

The fourth member of the group was a lean, dark-skinned man seated at the computer.

While Janek kept the four covered, Cade moved among them, disarming each after a thorough body search. He ejected the magazines from each weapon before tossing it into a waste bin beside Dekker's large desk.

"Keep the fingers off the keyboard," Janek called out to the computer operator.

"Move away, pal," Cade said. He caught hold of the man's collar and hauled him out of his seat, pushing him clear of the terminal. "I'd be disappointed if I thought you were going to clear that screen."

"Maybe I'd better take a look," Janek cautioned, crossing to sit at the terminal.

Cade ushered the four men across the office.

"So where do we go from here, Cade?" Brak asked. His voice held the trace of a sneer. He sounded like a man who still believed he held a winning hand.

"Back to New York," Cade said. "A lot of people have interest in you, Brak. And that doesn't include your ex-partners. They want you, as well, but for different reasons. I think you pissed them off."

"Shitheads," Brak said. "A bunch of no-hopers. They were going nowhere. So I helped 'em on their way," he added with a snigger.

"They won't be going as far as you, pal," Cade said. "Not all the way to Mars."

"Man has a sense of humor," Thornton said. "Mind he'll need it when I get him in my jail."

"I'll pass on that," Cade said.

"You dumb cop," Brak said. "You really think that Justice badge means a damn thing out here?"

Dekker managed a mirthless grin. "You ain't in the big city now, Cade. This is our territory. We run it and we make the rules."

Cade stared at the man. "Dekker, I've been making my own rules longer than you've had hairs on your fat ass!"

"Son of a bitch!" Thornton yelled, suddenly swinging around from Dekker's desk. His left arm came into view, a heavy onyx ashtray in his hand. Throwing the object at Cade, he lunged forward.

Cade twisted, his SMG's muzzle tracking away from the group as he arched his upper body away from the ashtray. It caught him on the right shoulder, and he gasped in pain. He sensed Thornton's heavy bulk looming close, felt the cop's thick shoulder slam into his chest. The force spun Cade across the room, bouncing him off the far wall.

Thornton, his beefy face stretched in a snarl, reached out with huge, clawing hands. One batted aside the SMG as the other groped for Cade's throat. Cade pulled back, feeling Thornton's fingers brush his flesh. Then he lashed out with the toe of his boot, whacking it up between Thornton's heavy thighs. The police chief uttered a screech. Cade shoved himself away from the wall, launching a hard fist that clouted Thornton under his wide, fleshy jaw. The meaty sound filled the room. Thornton slumped sideways, falling to his knees, head sagging. Blood began to dribble from his mouth where his teeth had snapped shut on his tongue.

Janek's response was swift and immediate. Rising, the cyborg reached the other three before Thornton had even struck Cade. Janek planted his tall frame in front of the three, the muzzle of his SMG unwavering.

"Not a chance in hell," he said with a benign smile on his face.

Bending over Thornton, Cade looped plastic cuffs around the crooked cop's thick wrists. "I'm running out of these damn things," he said.

"So let's shoot the rest of 'em," Janek offered. "Save everyone a deal of trouble."

Rubbing his sore shoulder, Cade crossed over to cuff Dekker, then the computer operator. "You got one for Mr. Brak?" Cade asked.

Janek tossed a plastic loop across to his partner, returning to the computer.

"Anything interesting on there?"

Janek gave a low chuckle. "Like winning the jackpot."

Cade finished cuffing the drug trafficker. He spun Brak around. "Where's Jessup?"

Brak maintained a poker face. "Who?"

"We had a make on your trigger before we left N.Y.," Janek said. "Want me to recite his rap sheet?"

"I don't know any Jessup."

"No? But I bet you're wishing he'd come through that door right now with that Casull autocannon."

Brak held Cade's rigid stare. The trafficker held out for almost a full minute before he switched his gaze, color rising in his cheeks.

"I love it when someone gives in gracefully," Cade said.

"Yes!" Janek whooped. "Yes, yes, yes."

"Don't fuse your chips," Cade said, leaning over his partner's shoulder. "What, already?"

"These turkeys have only put it all down for us," Janek explained. He pointed to names and locations on the monitor. "Delivery points. Distribution and local dealers from here to N.Y. and all points north and south. Brak's new setup, T.J."

"How you figure it's his new one?"

"Because the info I took from the memory back in N.Y. included a similar list. This is an updated one. Some of the locations are the same, but most of the dealer names are different. The new names will be to replace dealers from the old days who wouldn't play ball. Want to bet some of these names have been disappearing? Maybe turning up dead?"

"That the way it is, Brak?" Cade asked.

The trafficker gave a nervous laugh. "You don't know what you're talking about. You might as well let me go now, because there ain't enough to convict me of a damn thing."

"I'll take my chances," Cade said. He leaned forward so Brak could see his face clearly. "I can decide what to do on our way back to N.Y. Haul you in for trial or settle it on the road."

"What?" Brak frowned.

The computer operator cleared his throat nervously. "He's a Justice marshal, Brak. Hell, man, you know how they operate." The operator's face gleamed with sweat.

"Barranca, you keep your loose mouth shut," Brak snapped, lunging at the man.

"Or what?" Barranca asked. "You goin' to ice me, Brak? You don't, he will. Either way I ain't got much of a future, *compadre*. Eh? So screw you, Brak. You don't like it, sue me."

"Hell," Dekker said. "You can't trust anyone these days."

"Depressing, isn't it?" Janek said in a concerned tone. "Makes you wonder sometimes if it's all worth it."

The cyborg leaned over the keyboard, chuckling as he punched in the code for a full readout. "This is interesting, T.J."

Cade scanned the information on-screen. "They were the names you mentioned earlier. The financiers."

Janek pointed out numbers. "Bank deposit numbers. Names. Amounts. They tally with the numbers I decoded. Now follow this, T.J. Look at the amounts. Same amounts. But they've got a different number now. The same number.''

"Who the hell is this Harmon Lyall?"

"I have a feeling you've got him cuffed and ready for transit," Janek said quietly.

"Brak?"

Janek nodded. "If I have time, I'll pin down the location of this new account. Oh, and another thing. Brak has double-crossed the financiers, as well. He's transferred all their payoff money to a single account, under a false name."

"Just get that data locked away in your memory. I don't want to lose a single digit."

Janek raised his hand and wiggled his fingers. "Already done, Thomas. Would I ever be less than efficient?"

"In that case let's get the hell out of here before Jessup shows up. Our luck can't hold forever. We can go after him later."

"Back up to the roof?"

Cade nodded. "We'll grab one of those choppers and head for the airstrip." He indicated the text on the monitor. "Can you lose that stuff on-screen? Permanently. I don't want anyone else accessing it."

Janek's fingers made swift passes over the keyboard. He keyed in a number of overrides, cutting through the computer's data-protection shield.

"Hey, what's he doing?" Brak demanded, pushing toward the computer.

"This is legitimate business data," Dekker blustered. "I'll have my lawyer serve you so many writs you ain't goin' to have time to read 'em all."

"Dekker, shut up. Mister, you're busted, and you know it."

Cade snatched up the vid-phone, punching in a priority department code that connected him with Braddock's office in New York.

"T.J.? Where are you?" Braddock asked as his face appeared on the vid-screen.

"Kansas," Cade said. "And forget what Dorothy said, the yellow brick road doesn't take you to Oz."

He gave a brief rundown of events, bringing Braddock up to date with details of Mid State. "Get a local department team in here fast. I want this place shut down and searched. Tell the team they might have some resistance. There's a drug stash here somewhere. I don't want to risk losing my prisoners, so we're heading straight home."

"Don't get slack, T.J. It isn't over until it's finished," Braddock said.

"That man has a way with words," Janek muttered.

"I heard that," Braddock said.

The cyborg pulled a face, unseen by Braddock.

Cade cut the connection. He yanked the vid-phone's cord out of the wall junction box. Then he raised the SMG. "We are, as they say, out of here. Move it."

The group headed for the door. Janek hooked an arm under Thornton's and pulled the groggy cop to his feet. "Fresh air will clear your head, Chief," he said lightly.

Cade opened the door, checking the passage. Apart from the immobilized sec-droid, it was clear. "No hanging around, boys," he said.

Janek ushered the prisoners ahead of him up the roof stairs. Cade held back, watching the far end of the passage. Emerging on the roof, Janek herded the group across to the parked helicopters.

"Take Brak's chopper," Cade said. "Room for everyone in there."

Janek opened the hatch.

Cade started across to Thornton's police helicopter, intending to disable it.

He was reaching for the hatch access handle when a dark shadow fell across the chopper. Cade glanced skyward and saw another helicopter, slipping in silent mode toward the roof. It was a sleek, high-speed model, matt black and with an opaque canopy. The lowering sun threw vivid orange slashes of color over the burnished surfaces as the chopper swept in only feet above the roof.

Backing away from the police chopper, Cade yelled a warning, his eyes settling on the underslung rotary cannon fixed to the oncoming chopper.

The cannon's six barrels began to wink with spears of fire. Heavy-caliber shells pounded the roof, chewing ragged holes and filling the air with debris. The marching line of shells tore into the police chopper, shearing metal and plastic. Slivers flew in all directions. Cannon shells found the fuel tanks, and the blue-and-white chopper erupted in a fiery ball, spewing blazing fuel.

Cade felt the searing heat touch him as he hit the roof, bouncing and rolling, buffeted by the force of the blast.

The world was suddenly full of noise and color and heat. The cacophony overwhelmed him, yet he was still able to hear the high, wailing scream of someone in pain. Then even that sound was drowned by more cannon fire, the heavy, tearing racket numbing his eardrums.

He struggled to climb to his feet, feeling the impact of falling debris. He had barely regained his balance when a second explosion blew the day apart. Flame and smoke rolled across the roof. Knocked flat again, he lay half-conscious, stunned by the blast and choking on the drifting smoke. It hardly seemed worthwhile trying to stand up again—so he stayed the hell where he was.

"Let's go, Thomas! You can lie down all you want when you're dead! *Now move it!*"

Cade snapped out of the daze as Janek's voice boomed in his ear. He felt the cybo grab his arm and drag him to his feet.

The whole roof appeared to be on fire. Fuel from the burning helicopters had been sprayed in all directions, igniting and blazing fiercely. Thick smoke rolled from the shattered hulks of the wrecked machines. A scattering of debris was spread across the area. Most of it was from the machines.

Some was human.

Thornton and Dekker were down. Permanently, their bodies shredded and scorched, frozen in the rigid postures of death.

Barranca was on his knees, head down on his chest, moaning to himself as he clutched his shredded right arm. Blood was pulsing from his butchered shoulder, soaking his shirt. One side of his face was raw and blistered from the flames.

"Where's Brak?" Cade yelled above the noise.

Janek ignored him, half-dragging his partner across the roof, away from the carnage. The cyborg was aware of the attack chopper still around, hovering somewhere in the pall of smoke.

"Janek! Where is he?" Cade insisted.

"He ducked back inside," the cyborg replied. "Now keep moving, Thomas, I need my hands free."

Janek planted a hand between Cade's shoulders and shoved him between a couple of vent canopies. Turning, the cyborg swung his SMG into position, triggering a sustained burst at the attack chopper as it dropped into view again, swooping across the roof like a vulture, the rotary cannon loosing off streams of shells.

"Barranca! Move, man!" Janek yelled.

His words broke through too late. As Barranca stumbled to his feet, turning to run, he stepped directly into the path of the cannon fire. The stream of shells caught him and whipped his shuddering figure across the roof. Their destructive power chewed him apart. Gouts of bloody flesh and bone exploded from Barranca's body. The shells almost tore him in half, depositing his writhing, humping form facedown on the roof.

Turning sharply, the attack chopper pulled away as Janek's autofire laid a line of sparking hits along the lower fuselage.

"He'll be back," Janek said. "Inside, Thomas."

They broke for the access door.

As they neared it, the door burst open and a man appeared, opening fire with an autorifle.

Janek moved sideways as the stream of slugs whizzed over his head.

Before the gunner could alter his aim, Cade hit him, shoulder first, wrapping his arms around the guy's torso. The forward motion of his headlong charge took both men back through the door and down the inner stairs. As they hit bottom, Cade kicked free, rolling and regaining his feet, turning quickly to face the gunner.

Closing his fingers over the dropped autorifle, the gunner pulled the weapon close as he rose. Blood was trickling down the side of his face. He searched for Cade, eyes locking on the Justice cop.

Cade swung his booted foot in a looping arc. It smashed against the side of the gunner's head, slamming him to the floor. Cade snatched the autorifle, covering the passage as Janek followed him down the stairs.

"Brak came in here," Janek said. "He'll be trying to get out of the building."

"Let's go," Cade snapped, and made for the opposite end of the passage from Dekker's office.

A flight of stairs led to the floor below. They emerged on a wide landing with more passages leading to other offices. The landing had a longer flight of stairs leading to the ground floor. The reception area was almost deserted because of the gunfire and explosions.

Cade rushed downstairs, his rising anger fueled by the loss of his prisoner. He refused to give up on Brak. The trafficker was behind all the mayhem that had taken place from New York to Kansas. People were dead and Brak was responsible. Cade had no intention of allowing him to escape.

He burst out of the main doors. A parking lot spread out before him. Cars were being started as the evacuated people from the building tried to get clear. All they managed to do was create a noisy traffic snarl.

"See him?" Cade asked as Janek joined him.

The cybo scanned the parking lot. The light was fading now, shadows lengthening.

"There!" Janek said.

Cade followed his finger.

He saw Loren Brak on the east side of the lot. His hands cuffed behind his back, the trafficker was scrambling up a grassy bank, stumbling, falling, then clambering to his feet and running on.

"Go!" Cade yelled. "I'll cut around the other side."

Janek ran across the parking lot, dodging the moving cars with ease.

Skirting the edge of the lot, Cade tried to ignore the burning pain deep in his chest. His breathing was still labored from the smoke he'd inhaled.

Janek was closing fast, lessening the distance between himself and Brak.

The squeal of brakes alerted the cyborg to possible danger. A powerful Pontiac SportsBird Turbo roared along a feeder road on a line that would intersect with Brak.

Clearing the final row of parked vehicles, Janek hit the grassy bank. He pounded across it, angling toward Brak.

The Pontiac swung close to Brak, the passenger door opening. Brak, bending to climb into the car, paused to look over his shoulder. Not at Janek. The trafficker was looking above the cyborg's head.

Janek turned and saw the attack chopper diving from the graying sky. The cannon began to fire, shells chewing up the pavement just short of the Pontiac.

Janek shouldered the SMG and tracked the chopper. He fired off short bursts, laying his shots across the chopper's fuselage. Holding his ground, he fired again and again, seeing his shots strike the chopper. Suddenly trails of smoke emanated from the engine compartment. They grew thicker. Then the chopper's engine began to falter, the even sound turning ragged.

The chopper pulled up and away, curving out of range. It disappeared in the haze of smoke shrouding the roof of the Mid State building.

The screech of tires reached Janek's ears. He twisted around to see the Pontiac speeding toward the main highway. He could see that Cade had dropped to one knee, his autorifle up to his shoulder as the Pontiac raced along. The rifle jerked as he pumped shot after shot at the fleeing vehicle. The Pontiac swerved but maintained its speed. It bounced over the crest of the feeder road and disappeared from sight.

Janek felt a growing frustration. He stared at the spot where the car had vanished.

"Shit!" he exclaimed. "We blew it this time, partner. We really blew it."

10

Mid Town's police station was a square building, with the administration area occupying the upper two floors and the cells in the basement. The cells were filled with Mid Town's law force and some employees from Mid State Freight. Once news had leaked out that Chief Thornton and Dekker were dead, the Justice Department team from Kansas City had been swamped with information about who was involved in the drug dealing. It had been a night of confusion and bitterness. In Mid Town there was a great deal of resentment of Thornton's iron rule of law and Dekker's involvement with the traffickers. With the removal of the main oppressors, the floodgates had opened and information came thick and fast.

Jack Brink, the Kansas City Justice marshal, entered the office previously used by Chief Thornton and helped himself to a mug of coffee from the percolator.

"Damn good brew, T.J.," he said. "Thornton was a lousy cop but he had good taste in coffee."

Cade tossed down a sheaf of papers, arching his back. He pushed the comfortable recliner back from the desk and stood. Since the roof attack Cade and Janek had taken time to get themselves cleaned up and into some fresh clothes. Cade felt cosmetically better but was still aching from the physical effort. Plus, he was sore about losing Loren Brak.

"All this is great," he said. "But it isn't giving us a line on Brak's whereabouts."

"Goes with the territory," Brink said. "Major bust always generates paperwork. Tracking fugitives takes time."

"The longer it takes, the more likely he'll disappear."

Janek appeared in the doorway. "Just had a call from the highway patrol out near Quinn's Crossing. They've located the Pontiac."

"But no Brak?" Cade said.

Janek shook his head. "The car was burned out. Somebody had doused it in gas and set it alight." The cybo entered the office. "There was a corpse inside. Burned up pretty badly, but they've got an ID. It's Tate Jessup."

"Sounds odd," Brink said.

"Wait till you hear the rest," Janek said. "There were a couple of slugs in Jessup's back. Same caliber as the gun you used when firing at the car. Remember we saw it go off course for a few seconds."

"You must have hit him hard," Brink said.

"Not hard enough to kill him. He died from a bullet between the eyes. Different caliber."

"Who...?"

"Think about it, Jack. Brak and Jessup on the run. The last thing Brak would need to be hung with is a badly wounded man. What the hell could he do with Jessup? Take him to the nearest emergency hospital?

The man's on his way to a new life, ready to start up his drug empire somewhere on the West Coast. He's already proved he won't let anything stand in his way. Everyone's expendable—even his enforcer, once he's outlived his usefulness.''

Brink shook his head. "So the son of a bitch puts a slug in the guy's head, torches the car and takes off."

"Trying to cover his tracks. Jessup dead means he can't do any talking."

"What a mother," Brink said. He put down the mug of coffee. "Janek, where did that report say they found the car?"

"Quinn's Crossing. It's about two hundred miles west of here. Some little whistle-stop farming community."

"Yeah, I know it," Brink said. He crossed to the large map pinned to the wall behind the desk. "Here. Quinn's Crossing is right next to the main railroad link."

"Does that report give any indication when all this happened?" Cade asked.

"Not yet," Janek said. "But if I put through a call, maybe they can have it by the time we get there."

"Jack, Mid Town is all yours," Cade said.

"We've enough to keep us busy for a couple of days," Brink said. "Locating that cache of Thunder Crystals has cinched everything."

"Thanks for your help," Cade said. "Can you fix us with a ride so we can pick up our chopper?"

"Sure." Brink scooped up a key from the desk. "Why don't you take Thornton's truck? He isn't going to be needing it any longer."

JANEK TOOLED the powerful truck along the highway. Mid Town slipped out of sight in the dust clouding up from the rear wheels. It was an hour after daylight. The sun was already turning the new day hot.

"What's bugging you?" the cyborg asked after a lengthy silence.

"That damn chopper," Cade said. "I want to know who and why."

"I've been thinking about it myself. The only answer I came up with was Brak's ex-partners."

"Or some new players," Cade suggested.

"For example?"

"Brak's partners are pissed off, sure. But are they mad enough to want to kill Thornton? The guy who ran Mid Town for them? And Dekker?"

"So they found out the pair had sold them down the river. That was bound to give them enough incentive, Thomas."

"Maybe. But they'd have to be damn certain before they did it. And from what we've heard, Lorenzo and Shultz have been too busy saving their own hides to do much about Brak the last couple of days."

"You said new players. Who, exactly?"

"The people who can't afford to have the finger pointed at them. Now the Outfit's been broken up, they'll want out with their reputations unstained. And they won't be too happy about Brak running off with their cut of the loot."

"The city financiers. I think you might have a point there, T.J. They won't feel happy until the whole organization has been wiped out. A total cover-up."

"And that could include Lorenzo and Shultz," Cade added.

He reached for the handset and punched in a number.

Braddock's voice grated over the line. "Yeah?"

"Cade. I need a question answered."

"Shoot."

"Any reports on Lorenzo or Shultz?"

"Matter of fact, yes," Braddock said. "They're both dead. We got the report a while ago. Explains why we couldn't find them. Apparently they were found together in Lorenzo's car upstate. Parked near a deserted gas station. The car was riddled with cannon fire. And so were Lorenzo and Shultz. The way the report reads, they must have been waiting for someone. There was no sign of any disturbance. The angle of the cannon fire suggests the attack was from the air. We figure somebody set them up, T.J. Arranged a meet, then shot them to death. Looks like Brak got his wish. Now all his partners are dead."

"Might be what he wished, but I don't think he fixed this particular hit," Cade said. "We've got a wild card in the deck. He's already showed his hand. We had Brak, the local renegade police chief and the head man of Mid Town ready for transportation last night. Before we could take them away, we were hit with cannon fire from a chopper."

"You guys okay?"

"Sure," Cade replied. "Except our pride got dented. We ended up with a bunch of dead prisoners and Loren Brak running free and clear."

"You sure it wasn't Brak's people freeing him?"

"Not the way that chopper was spraying us with cannon shells. They wanted us all dead. Brak included."

"Any notion who?"

"Suspicions. But I need more proof."

Braddock sighed. "I'll leave it with you, T.J. What's your next move?"

"We've got a line on Brak, so we're following it up. On our way to pick up our chopper, then we're heading west. Be in touch."

Cade hung up the handset. "Janek, for Christ's sake put the pedal to the floor. You're driving like we were on a Sunday outing."

The cybo responded. The truck leaped forward, burning rubber.

Cade stared through the fly-speckled windshield. He was thinking about three dead Justice marshals and one dead enforcer by the name of Tate Jessup. At least that part of the deal had been settled. Jessup might have died at someone else's hand, but at least he'd paid the price. It was only satisfactory in a distant way, as far as Cade was concerned, but he realized that under the circumstances it was the best he was liable to get.

THE HIGHWAY PATROLMAN who had found the car took Cade and Janek to view the burned-out Pontiac. It had been parked in a hollow off the highway a couple of miles outside Quinn's Crossing.

The officer behind the cruiser's wheel was a lean, sandy-haired youngster, more than eager to help in what he saw as a major incident.

"She was burning pretty fierce when I rolled by," he explained. "Must have been going for a good while. Too damn hot for me to get near. All I could do was call in the fire department, then sit and wait."

"Were there any reports of unusual incidents last night?" Janek asked. "Gunshots?"

"No, sir, Marshal Janek," the patrolman said. "Not likely to be out here. There aren't any houses out this way. Gets pretty lonely after dark. We wouldn't have spotted the burning car if'n it hadn't been on my regular patrol."

"Stolen cars? Rentals?" Janek asked.

"No, sir. I checked that myself."

Cade was checking a map of the area. "It's more than likely Brak headed for the railroad. If he could pick up a local, he'd be able to reach a main line station and jump one of the cross-country flyers."

"Be easy enough," the patrolman said. "Automated service runs twenty-four hours. He picked up one of those, he'd be in Topeka in a couple of hours."

"I'm going for that," Cade said. "It'd be Brak's easiest way out. He'd go for the ride that attracted the least attention. He's got us chasing him and this guy in the chopper. He wants to hit L.A. and lose himself."

The highway patrolman said, "You sayin' he *wants* to go to Los Angeles? Hell, he must be crazy."

"If he is, we're just as bad," Janek remarked, "'cause that's exactly where we have to go to catch him."

"Nobody said the job had to be fun all the time," Cade remarked.

THERE WAS A MESSAGE waiting for Cade to call Jack Brink when they got back their chopper.

"T.J., we got something that could tie in to the hit last night."

"Shoot."

"We found the chopper, abandoned about five miles the other side of Mid Town. It took a number of shots through a pressure line. We found tire tracks nearby. Must have been a pickup car waiting for them. It headed cross-country. We followed, but the trail petered out after a few miles."

"Get anything from the chopper?"

"The one bright spot, T.J. We found some prints inside. I'm running them through Washington Central right now. Soon as I get a readout, I'll let you have it."

"Appreciate that, Jack."

"What about your burnout?"

"Confirmation that the body belongs to Jessup. No sign of Brak, but we're pretty certain he's on his way to L.A. By train."

"He's nothing if not versatile."

"I'd go for a pain in the ass, Jack."

"Talk to you later, T.J."

AN HOUR LATER, with the helicopter fueled up, Cade and Janek were back in the air. Janek punched in a course for Los Angeles via the Washington Central computer. Once it was locked into the chopper's system, Janek keyed in the autopilot and sat back in his reclining seat. He closed his eyes, flicking through the radio dial, and relaxed as he picked up a jazz broadcast.

Cade picked up the handset and punched in a number. "T. J. Cade," he said when the connection was made. "Patch me through to the L.A. department office."

"One moment," the female operative in Washington Central advised.

Cade leaned back, scanning the chopper's instrument layout. The craft was maintaining its course at a steady altitude. The computer's sensors, situated on the chopper's outer skin, monitored any changes and relayed them to the inbuilt program, which made the necessary changes to the flight pattern. Extreme changes would activate a warning, both visual and audible, bringing the human—cyborg, in Janek's case—pilot back to the controls.

"Marshal Cade? This is Hal Jordan, L.A. Justice Department. What can I do to help you?"

Cade sketched in the background to the case. "Right now Brak is heading your way. I'm certain he's coming in by train. But knowing the way he thinks, he could ditch that and change to something else for the last part of the journey."

"I'll pull Brak's file and issue a search-and-seize order for him. We've a good number of enforcement agencies out here. I'll ask for cooperation and have them go on lookout. All we can do is cover every means of entry into California and try to pick Brak up before he reaches Los Angeles. If he does hit the city, it's going to be a lot harder. You familiar with this burg?"

"Only by what I see on TV."

Jordan laughed. "You're in for a shock, Cade. California's a hell of a place. It's great but it's crazy, too.

Hope you enjoy your stay. Let me know when you arrive. I'll assign a couple of my people to give you an assist. In the meantime I'll put the word out on the street. See if anyone has heard about this new drug setup.''

Cade replaced the handset. He glanced at Janek, still seemingly lost in his jazz music.

''California?'' the cyborg muttered in disgust, showing he had been listening to Cade's conversation. ''Fantasy land, T.J. Full of oranges, movie studios and crazy people.''

''And now Loren Brak.''

''There's a bright side to it,'' Janek said. ''They're getting us, too.''

Los Angeles

They entered Los Angeles airspace midmorning the following day. Within minutes the L.A. Air Control Department came through on the radio.

"Please identify yourself. We have you on-screen. Your registration is out of state."

"L.A. Control, this craft is registered to the Justice Department, New York City." Janek activated the computer code that would flash their official ID on the air controller's screen.

"Acknowledged. Welcome to the Los Angeles area. Have you a destination? Or would you like a guide drone to assist?"

"Thank you, no," Janek said. "We're headed for the Justice Department at New Parker Center. They have already been notified of our arrival."

"Thank you for your cooperation," the controller said.

"Well, they're very polite," Janek said.

As the chopper swept in over the vast sprawl of Los Angeles, the city's immense size showed itself.

L.A. lay beneath a soft haze made semitransparent by the sun. The city seemed to go on forever in every direction, and as Janek took the chopper down they were able to make out the intricate web of freeways and interconnecting ramps. The L.A. transport system, developed over the decades, gave substance to the myth of the California car cult. Despite the advances of air cruisers, the Californians still revered their ground-based vehicles, which had proliferated by the thousands. Land had been claimed by the government from time to time in order to add yet more freeways. If extra land wasn't available, then new highways were built over existing ones, creating multilayer systems. This happened frequently within the city areas, where freeways curved and rose between and over whole city blocks.

Even the skies over L.A. were crowded. Advertising drones, floating platforms carrying huge vid-screens, air-lane markers—they all cluttered the hazy emptiness. Air cruisers of various sizes and shapes slid back and forth.

It was all watched over by the ever-present LAPD air cruisers and helicopters.

Dropping down toward the imposing, reconstructed New Parker Center, the Justice cops viewed the L.A. skyline with mixed feelings. The California architecture was way ahead of anything New York had to offer, but Cade felt it lacked something. There were too many cold steel and plasglass constructions for Cade's liking. New York, for all its advances, still maintained a great deal of its old character. Los Angeles, if it had ever had character, appeared to have abandoned it for the pristine look of the electronic age.

California had long since succumbed to the lure of the microchip. It intruded into every aspect of life, benefiting in many instances, but dominating in others. Automation was the name of the game, spearheaded by the vast Japanese-owned megacorporations that had increased their dominance by leaps and bounds since the turn of the century. Money and power, always at the forefront of California dreaming, had tipped the scales, creating a state that relied heavily on the wonders of electronic aids and devices.

Janek touched down on the vast rooftop helipad of the Parker Center. The radio chattered and warbled to itself, an array of speech patterns running through complicated checks and analysis of the helicopter's condition. By the time Cade and Janek climbed from the chopper, it was surrounded by a collection of automated machines, intent on fully servicing and maintaining its efficiency.

"I'm beginning to dislike this place already," Janek grumbled, stepping clear of the whirring, busy machines.

"Stay with it, partner," Cade said. "It can only get worse," he added with a smirk.

They were confronted by a slender, gleaming silver android. The droid inclined its naked, polished skull.

"Marshal Cade. Marshal Janek. Please follow me. I will take you to meet Hal Jordan." Its voice was low and gentle, the words clear and polite.

The droid turned and walked away, gesturing with a slender, chromed arm. "I hope you had a pleasant trip.

Flying these days can be such a strain, don't you agree?''

Cade saw the disgusted look on Janek's face. The cyborg hated the kind of sycophancy demonstrated by the hospitality droid. Service droids in general, who had a single function—to please humans in whatever capacity their programming instructed—went against Janek's independent line of thought. Even though he accepted that they couldn't do anything else because of their design, he felt that type of behavior denigrated all droids.

An express elevator took them down to the Justice Department floor of the spacious building. It had been built on the site of the original Parker Center, expanded to cover almost six times the area, and now incorporated half a dozen law-enforcement agencies within its miles of corridors and acres of floor space.

The L.A. Justice Department looked more like a spacious, modern hotel than a law department. The order and near silence of the place were nothing like the hectic atmosphere of the New York offices. And the personnel all looked like TV stars. Everyone had a tan and seemed to be blond and lean.

"They get all these out of the same mold?" Janek asked.

"Hal Jordan's office, gentlemen," the droid said as it opened the door and ushered them in. It waited until the door had closed before falling into immobility, waiting for its next set of instructions.

HAL JORDAN WAS as tall as Cade. He had light blond hair above a strong, tanned, open face.

"Sit down," he said, indicating the comfortable recliners.

"You got anything for us?" Cade asked.

Jordan smiled. He had been warned about Cade's direct, no-nonsense approach.

"We've done our best, Cade," he said, reaching for a file. He pulled out a few sheets, glancing at them briefly to acquaint himself with the contents before passing them to Cade.

Janek leaned over to scan the sheets as Cade worked through them. The cyborg had completed reading them well ahead of his human partner.

"A few hints, but nothing substantial," Jordan admitted. "The street's always buzzing with talk. It's a busy world out there. We've got a big city to cover. L.A. county covers one hell of a chunk of real estate."

Cade finished reading and dropped the sheets back onto Jordan's desk, a grunt of annoyance passing his lips. "He's here somewhere," he said tautly. "And I want him."

"I said I'd get someone to work with you," Jordan said. "I've assigned one of my best teams. Wexler and Paris."

"A local team could help, T.J.," Janek said pleasantly, sensing Cade's impatience. "They'll know the best places to go for information. Save us time."

Cade didn't answer. He was gazing around Jordan's office. It was an attempt to distance himself from the heat of the moment. He knew he was being unreasonable. Jordan had done everything he could. It wasn't for Cade to judge the man too harshly.

"Wexler, you want to come into my office," Jordan said into his communicator. He flipped the button and leaned back in his recliner. A quick smile crossed his lips. "How's New York these days?"

"I'd say rough and messy describes it," Janek informed him. "It's starting to go at the seams, but no one's ready to stand up and say so."

"L.A. without the smog is all," Jordan said. "I was in N.Y. for six months way back. It was hard then, but it's still a hell of a town."

"Hasn't changed much," Janek confirmed.

The door opened and Wexler and Paris stepped inside. Wexler was a tall, athletic blonde. His blue eyes and strong white teeth were accentuated by his deep tan. He wore a bright sports shirt and tan slacks. His shoulder rig held a sleek SIG-Sauer 9 mm autopistol.

Janek allowed him a passing glance. He was more interested in his partner.

The moment Paris entered the office, Janek knew she was a cyborg. Paris was Janek's height, less an inch or so. Built on sleek, shapely lines, the female cyborg had a shaped cap of chestnut-colored hair and deep green eyes. Her flesh tone was a soft, tawny hue that emphasized her flushed, curving lips. Paris wore slim-fit pants and a clinging roll-neck sweater under a tailored jacket.

Jordan made the introductions.

"Call me Jerry," Wexler said, reaching for Cade's hand. "I hear you've had a hard time on this one."

"You could say that," Cade admitted. "I'd be worried if every perp we went after gave up without a struggle."

Wexler gave a brittle laugh. He sounded a little up-tight, as though the idea of a partnership, albeit a short one, didn't sit too easily on his broad, tanned shoulders.

Paris closed the door, turning smoothly. "I've been doing a little checking on my own," she said. Her voice was low and controlled, with a soft huskiness that made it very appealing. "The main drug organizations in the area are controlled by three racial groups—the Hispanic groups, the Caribbean cartels and the Oriental. Loren Brak doesn't belong to any of them so he'll be looking for a minority organization. The fact that he has the formulation for the Thunder Crystals gives him an edge. It puts him in a strong bargaining position."

"Have you found anything?" Janek asked, failing to keep the admiration out of his voice.

Paris nodded. "Yes. I checked with some of our info peddlers. Early this morning I received a call from one. The word's going round about an auction among the smaller drug groups. Our peddler seems to think there's a new man in town with a hot deal."

"You kept that quiet," Wexler said tightly.

Paris glanced at him, faintly smiling. "I tried to catch you at your apartment, but you weren't there. First time I saw you this morning was on the way up to the office."

"Yeah, well, I had a busy night." Wexler grinned.

"You live separately?" Janek asked.

Paris nodded. "California passed the Robotics Equality Bill last year," she said. "It allows for independent existence."

"That sounds really interesting," Janek said, nudging Cade in the ribs. "What do you say, T.J.? Can I leave home and get my own place? Pretty please?"

Paris laughed softly at Cade's scowl.

"I might just take you up on that, Janek," he said.

"So," Wexler interrupted, "how do you want to handle this, Cade?"

"We need to get out on the street and do some pushing. Sitting around isn't going to do it."

"Fine by me," Wexler said brightly. "Let's go check out some transport."

He nodded to Jordan. "See you, boss. Let's go, folks. We've a lot of sights to see."

IN THE LARGE ELEVATOR on the way down to the basement parking area, Janek stood beside Paris.

"I'm intrigued by this independent living style, Paris," he said.

The cyborg glanced at him. "I take it you live with Cade?"

"We have an apartment in New York. Works out pretty well. I have my own room. Gives me privacy if I want it, and it allows T.J. his. He has a lady friend."

Paris smiled warmly. "Human relationships. It's something unique to them. Something we can't feel."

Janek kept his mouth shut. As much as he had taken to Paris, it didn't seem wise to voice his own personal feelings toward Dr. Abby Landers. He felt safer having told only Cade. His human partner, for all his weird sense of humor, was totally trustworthy.

They reached the basement. Wexler led them to the Justice Department car pool, where a skinny droid came hurrying across. It waved a finger at Wexler.

"No more damaged vehicles, Wexler," it shrilled. "How do you expect me to keep justifying all the repair work?"

Wexler smiled lamely. "Sorry about this."

Paris stepped in quickly, smiling sweetly at the droid.

The droid turned to glare at her. "You can quit that, too, Marshal Paris. I've fallen for your smooth tongue too many times. The word is no more damage. You think the department is made of money?"

Janek leaned forward to tap the droid on its polished shoulder. "You pay for them yourself, then?" he asked.

The droid stared at him blankly. "Damn stupid question. You know droids don't get paid."

"Fine," Janek said gently. Then he raised his voice. "So get the damn car and quit moaning over something that's got nothing to do with you!"

The droid scuttled off to pick out a vehicle.

"And make it a good one!" Janek threw at him.

"I'm impressed," Paris said.

"I'm curious," Cade said. "Hey, is that what you do with our droid back home?"

Janek gave a lopsided shrug.

The droid returned with an almost brand-new Corvette Lash, a sleek, powerful auto painted brilliant red.

Janek climbed in the back along with Paris, leaving Cade to join Wexler in the front.

"Let's go," Janek said breezily. "T.J., I'm starting to like California."

"Don't get too thrilled," Cade told him. "New York is still our beat."

"For now," Wexler said, "let me show you mine."

WEXLER WEAVED through the heavy traffic, cutting back and forth between lanes. He drove fast but well, enjoying the power of the Corvette. The day was heating up. Overhead the hazy blue sky, with a few scraps of white cloud, was thick with craft of every shape and size.

"Airspace is becoming a problem," Wexler said. "Everybody wants their own cruisers now they're so damn efficient. Trouble is they make a hell of a mess when they crash."

He flicked on the radio. Janek leaned forward as he caught the tones of a jazz combo.

"You like jazz?" Paris asked.

"He's a damn nut," Cade told her. "Listens to it all the time."

"Cool," Paris said. "Jazz is very...very..." She peered at Janek, who had turned to watch a helicopter that appeared to be flying parallel with them. "Janek?"

The cyborg raised a hand to silence her, activating his vision enhancer.

Wexler cut the music as the communicator radio crackled into life.

"Call for Marshal Cade."

Cade picked up the handset. "Cade here."

"Message from your department in New York, Marshal. Fingerprints found in the helicopter used in the attack at Mid Town belong to Earl Prochek, known merchandiser of illegal goods. Your people tracked him down and put the frighteners on him. He hadn't realized how deep in he was. Someone promised him a trip to Mars if he didn't do some talking. He came up with the name of the man to whom he supplied the chopper. Fellow named Ryker. No first name—just Ryker. Mean anything to you?''

"Damn right," Cade answered. "Ryker is one of the top hired assassins on the Eastern Seaboard. His price is high, too damn high for most. But he's good. Nothing he won't do for the right amount of cash."

"Something else, Marshal," the dispatcher said. "The service droids checking your helicopter found an electronic tracking device fixed under the body. Looks like someone wanted to keep an eye on you."

"Thanks for the info," Cade said. He replaced the handset. "You hear that, partner?" he asked.

"Affirmative," Janek said. "Wexler, can you get us to some kind of cover?"

"Cover? What cover?"

"Wexler, just get us off this damn freeway!" Paris yelled. She had picked up on Janek's unease. "I think we have an airborne tail."

Cade twisted around in his seat, following Janek's gaze.

"There," Janek said. "And he isn't waiting to be invited."

The distant chopper suddenly dropped, curving down in a long dive, angling across the hazy sky.

Wexler swung the Corvette across the lanes of moving traffic toward the nearest off ramp. Leaving a trail of screeching tires as drivers braked, the Corvette hit the ramp at a rising fifty. The car bounced wildly, fishtailing for long yards as Wexler hung on to the wheel.

The hostile chopper came streaking across the empty sky, rocking slightly as the pilot settled his craft for its hit.

"The mother!" Cade mouthed as he thrust a hand under his jacket, closing his fist around the butt of his Magnum.

"Heads down," Janek suggested, spotting the brief flash of a launching missile as he yanked out his auto-pistol.

The rocket whizzed over the Corvette and buried itself in the embankment slope running alongside the off ramp. The explosion sent a boiling sphere of fire and smoke lashing back at the Corvette. The heat wave seared the car's paintwork. The racket of the explosion washed over the car's occupants.

For a few seconds Wexler lost control. But he forced himself to haul in on the wheel, pulling the Corvette back on line. He jammed his foot down, sending the car surging up the ramp.

"Too damn open," Cade yelled. "We're still exposed."

The chopper let go a second and third missile moments before it overflew them and banked sharply to the crackle of Janek's handgun.

The final rocket hit the off ramp by the rear fender. The blast lifted the vehicle off its rear wheels and slammed it against the embankment. The car bounced as it struck, still pushing forward until the nose buried itself in the soft earth, then it shuddered to a groaning halt, throwing the occupants from their seats.

Janek kicked open the door, reaching across to grab Cade by the collar and haul him out.

Wexler had already rolled out his own sprung door, landing hard. He scrambled to his feet, Paris on his heels, following Janek and Cade along the ramp.

"I smell gas," Janek warned.

A moment later the Corvette was enveloped in a rolling mass of flame as the spilled fuel ignited, streaking for the ruptured tank and blowing it wide open. The blast slammed them all to the ground, heat washing over them.

"He's on his way back," Paris called out, pulling her handgun from its hip holster under her jacket.

The attack chopper had completed its curve and had leveled out, sweeping up the ramp no more than a few feet from the surface.

As it loomed ever larger, bearing down on the group of Justice cops, the underslung rapid-fire cannon opened up again, laying down a deadly stream of howling shells.

12

"Damn it to hell!"

Cade's anger blasted from his lips. He gripped his powerful Magnum autopistol in both hands and leveled it at the chopper, shimmering through the haze of cannon fire shredding the road.

"Thomas, get your ass out of there!" Janek yelled.

"I've had it with these scumbags!" Cade screamed.

He triggered a volley of steady shots at the canopy of the chopper as it zoomed up the off ramp. He never did know whether he made any hits. Janek struck him in a flying tackle seconds before the chopper reached him. The pair crashed to the ground in a cloud of dust and flying stone chips, the roar of the chopper drowning Cade's wild yell of frustration.

"Shit, Janek, I had the bastard in my sights!" Cade raged as he struggled to his feet, streaked with dust. "When are you going to stop interfering?"

Knocking the dust from his clothing, Janek raised his head. "When you quit playing around like a damn rookie."

"Me?"

"I'm not talking to anyone else, Thomas. And quit shouting. I'm not deaf."

"Dumb is what you are."

Cade scanned the hazy sky for the chopper. It had circled in a wide curve, and Cade watched it slip lazily back down through the empty void on a return run.

"The son of a bitch is coming back. So how do we get out of this one, supercop?"

Janek ignored the jibe. "We make a tactical withdrawal," he said. "In your words, Thomas, we run like our asses are alight."

"Sounds good to me," Wexler said.

They turned and struck out along the embankment, angling toward the crest. The chopping crackle of cannon fire reached their ears before they were halfway there. Gouts of earth flew into the air from the cannon shells.

"Scatter!" Cade yelled above the racket. "Spread out!"

Each of the four moved in a different direction.

The thunder of the cannon fire and the roar of the chopper's powerful engine drowned out every other sound. Dust and shredded grass swirled around them, buffeted by the rotor wash. The wind tugged at their clothing and physically pushed them across the slope as the chopper swung in low, the hatches in the fuselage sliding open to expose the gunners waiting to fire.

Janek, swinging around, his autopistol gripped two-handed, triggered fast shots at one of the gunners. The volley cut ragged holes in his upper body, twisting him around. As he fell, the gunner's skull smacked against the edge of the open hatch. His body dangling by the safety belt anchoring him to the chopper's frame, his autorifle slipped from his dead fingers.

Hearing the sharp crackle of small-caliber autofire, Wexler glanced over his shoulder, spotting the gunner on his side. The Justice cop threw up his handgun, triggering a rapid trio of shots that clanged against the chopper's outer skin, close to the open hatch. Pulling back, the gunner braced himself and returned fire.

Wexler gave a hoarse grunt as several slugs tore into his chest. He fell over backward, losing his weapon, and slithered down the slope.

Paris saw him go down. She crossed over to him and knelt beside him, protecting his body with her own, tracking the swaying chopper with her autopistol. The cyborg triggered fast, accurate shots, laying a tight grouping over the gunner's chest. The guy's body exploded with pain. Blood began to blossom across his chest as he slumped to the floor of the chopper.

Crouching, Cade fixed his Magnum on the chopper's canopy. His eyes narrowed against the flying dust, he gripped the weapon with both hands and held steady. He picked up the rising pitch in the chopper's engine as the pilot poured on the power for a getaway.

"No way, pal," Cade murmured, and opened fire. He triggered carefully, holding down the Magnum's recoil, putting each shot through the canopy where he figured the pilot was sitting.

Several of the high-velocity slugs penetrated the plasglass and found their intended target. The chopper suddenly sideslipped, losing power. It swung in a lazy half circle before the underbelly ploughed into the embankment. The chopper hit the earth with a solid crunch. As it tilted to one side, the whirling rotors sliced into the dirt, stalling the engine and bringing the machine to a final, shuddering halt. Broken shards of the rotor blades whirled through the air. Curls of white vapor seeped through the vent holes over the engine compartment.

"Look after Wexler," Cade called to Paris, and took off after his partner.

Janek was leaning through the open hatch, unclipping the safety belt of the gunner Paris had shot. The guy was moaning, eyes rolling as Janek picked him up and carried him out.

"Stay back, T.J., that chopper's going to blow," Janek warned.

They moved down the slope. Paris was ahead of them, carrying Wexler's limp form.

"That was good shooting, T.J.," Janek said.

"Yeah. I know."

Janek shook his head. "My partner. Modest to the last."

The chopper exploded with a huge noise, sending a swirl of flame skyward. It engulfed the chopper in an instant.

By the time they reached her, Paris was talking into a compact walkie-talkie, requesting backup and medical assistance. She was kneeling beside Wexler. The Justice cop lay still, his eyes closed. Paris rose, turning to face Cade and Janek.

"He's dead," she said calmly. "I tried to help, but the bullets had done too much damage. Wasn't anything I could do."

"Damn," Cade said wearily. He turned away, searching his pockets for a cigar. The one he found was crushed, but he lit it anyway. He sat down on the embankment and waited for the backup to arrive.

Paris watched Janek place the wounded perp on the grass. The guy had opened his eyes. He stared at the impassive cyborgs and reminded himself they were only machines, without feelings. The more he thought about that, the less secure he felt.

"Is he the one I shot?" Paris asked.

Janek nodded.

"So he killed Wexler," Paris remarked. The cybo knelt beside the wounded man. "You hear that? You just killed my partner. The only partner I ever had."

The perp, hurting from his wounds and nervous at being confronted by the cyborg cop, gazed around with wide eyes.

"Someone hired you for this," Paris continued. "I need to know who. Very badly."

"So?"

"So if you believe you're hurting as bad as you can—think again."

Paris laid a slender finger over one of the perp's bullet wounds and pressed gently.

The guy gasped, sweat popping out on his face. "This ain't legal," he protested. "I got my rights."

Paris shook her head. "I'm a Justice marshal. My rulebook says different."

Before even Janek could do a thing, Paris slammed her clenched fist against the perp's bloody chest, wrenching a terrified scream from him as his body arched in pain.

"Make or break, you bastard. Now give me a name."

"Paris!" Janek said, leaning over to grab her arm. "Not this way."

The cyborg turned to him, face hardened with bitterness, eyes glittering with a ferocity he had never encountered in his kind before.

"Don't interfere, Janek. Not this time." Her voice had flattened, losing the gentleness it had held before. It was without warmth or feeling, simply a mechanical tone that betrayed Paris's birthright.

Returning to the moaning perp, Paris leaned in close, letting him see her bloody fist. "Your memory any better?"

"Ryker," the perp whispered through clenched teeth. "La Rosa motel on the Malibu Strip. Cabin 18. Now get the fuck away from me, you android bitch."

Paris stood, smiling gently at Janek. Once again the soft gleam filled her blue eyes and her features had softened.

"Don't take it to heart, Janek," she said pleasantly. "All in a day's work. You know that old saying— 'Different strokes for different folks.' And it got us what we wanted, didn't it?"

Janek watched her walk away, moving to meet the first of the L.A. highway patrol air cruisers as it coasted down. The distant wail of approaching sirens filled the air.

"They breed 'em tough out here, partner," Cade said as he fell in beside Janek.

"I don't believe I like that kind of tough," Janek said.

"It's the difference between male and female," Cade said. 'Paris just saw her partner killed. Her programming caused her to react from the female perspective. They get very protective where partners of any kind are concerned."

Janek watched an L.A. County ambulance cruiser sink to the ground. The rear door swung open to allow the med-droids to emerge. They were dressed in spotless white jumpsuits, their chrome skulls polished to a high shine.

"Would you expect me to react that way if you got killed?"

"If I was dead, I wouldn't give a damn what you did," Cade said. "This is getting too technical for me. Bring it up next time you have a session with Abby Landers. She'll explain it better than I can."

"I've called for an unmarked air cruiser," Paris said as she rejoined them. "I take it you want to hit the motel."

Cade nodded. "Sooner the better. If Ryker's on a roll, I want to be close behind him. Right now he's our only chance of a lead to Brak."

"That's true, T.J., he is doing better than we are at the moment," Janek said.

"Ryker has the advantage of having money, muscle and a direct involvement. It's his profession and he has to show results. So he uses different ways to get his answers. And he's known by the people he's dealing with. Ryker has a bad reputation. He'll kill just to find out the time of day. People tend to talk under that kind of pressure."

"I thought we were supposed to be heavy-handed, T.J.?"

"There's a cutoff point for us, partner. Not for Ryker."

ONE OF THE OLDER motel complexes, La Rosa had sprung up on the Malibu Strip alongside the main highway during the boom just after the war. California had been lucky. No missiles or pollution had reached the West Coast state. Subsequently there had been a heavy influx of immigrants. After a year the Californian authorities clamped down on the steady stream of people trying to enter the state. The ban had slowed the flood but had failed to stop it entirely.

Since then the Malibu Strip had degenerated into a tacky few miles of massage parlors, convenience stores, porno houses and cheap hotels and motels. It had an unsavory reputation but was also fairly resilient to change. It offered a place to stay for those who had little hope of finding anywhere else.

Or for those who wanted somewhere away from prying eyes and questions.

Paris put the unmarked cruiser down on a strip across the three-lane highway from La Rosa. The motel stood back from the highway. It was a collection of dilapidated cabins connected by covered walkways. Near the central office, which also held a store and launderette, was a parking lot and gas station.

"I've seen better," Janek said after casting an eye over the layout.

"The strip is going through hard times," Paris offered. "Business is bad."

They climbed from the cruiser. Paris closed the hatch and locked it down. Crossing the highway, they skirted the office and cut through to the first cabin. Paris indicated the numbers painted on its side. "Should be at the far end of this row," she said.

Cade pulled his Magnum, holding the weapon out of sight against his leg. "We need information," he said. "Not dead bodies."

The cabins had a front entrance only. There were two windows on the front wall, two more on the back.

"Paris, cover the rear. I want you backing me when I go in, Janek."

"Let's do it," Janek said.

Cade eased around the wall, flattening against the frontage. He crouched below the window, waiting by the door until Janek was beside him. Then he quickly moved to the other side of the entrance, turned and kicked the flimsy door open with the sole of his boot. Ducking, he went in fast, breaking to the right, his Magnum thrust out in front of him.

There was sudden movement in the dim room. On one side of the room, a man cursed. On the other side, a chair crashed to the floor. The thunder of a shot filled the room, the muzzle-flash bright in the shadows. The slug tore through the wall behind Cade, allowing a thin shaft of sunlight to penetrate.

Cade dropped to a crouch, searching for a target. He saw the dark outline of the gunman as he turned his powerful handgun toward Cade. The Justice cop triggered a slug into the guy's leg, knocking him across the room.

On the tail of Cade's shot a second shot sounded as Janek picked up the room's other occupant. The man had been reaching for a shotgun when Janek blew a fist-sized hole through his left shoulder. He gave a startled scream and stumbled back, tripping across a low table.

Cade pushed upright, scanning the room.

The shadows were abruptly banished as Janek raised the blinds.

"Shut the door," Cade ordered. He crossed the room, picking up discarded weapons. Only then did he check out the wounded perps.

"Shall I call in a med-team?" Janek asked.

"Yeah, go ahead."

"And make it quick," one of the perps said angrily.

"Maybe I shouldn't," Janek suggested. "Looks like we got a hardass who wants to tough it out. What do you say, T.J.?"

Cade stood over the man Janek had shot in the shoulder. He was a lean brown guy with shoulder-length blond hair and a tattooed face. The perp glared up at Cade, teeth gritted against the pain from his shattered shoulder. His hand was clamped over the ragged wound, and blood was seeping through his fingers.

"Ryker must be down on his luck having to hire you dope-heads."

"Yeah? Go screw yourself, cop. So you got me and Slick. I'll piss on your grave when Ryker gets done with ya."

"He must be in love with the guy," Cade said.

Cade turned at the sound of Paris's voice calling his name. There was something in her tone that brought a chill to his gut.

"Keep an eye on this pair," he said.

Janek, on the vid-phone, raised a hand in acknow-
ledgment.

Paris had climbed through one of the rear bathroom windows. She was standing at the door to the
bathroom.

"In here, Cade. But it isn't very pleasant."

Standard for a cheap motel, the bathroom was a tiled
room containing a toilet, washbasin and shower unit.
The tiles were white, giving the place a cold, clinical
feel. Almost like an operating room, Cade thought as
he stepped inside, and recoiled at what he saw.

"Jesus Christ!"

The white tiles were splashed with blood. It seemed
to be everywhere, especially around the shower, from
which the naked, butchered corpse of a man hung.
He'd been strung up by a length of electrical cable
looped beneath his arms and then secured to the shower
fixture, and his face and body had been deliberately
and deeply cut and sliced. Someone had tortured the
man, killing him slowly and very painfully. Carving
him up so that he died in gruesome agony. Pools of
blood had congealed in the shower tray below the dangling corpse.

"I know this one," Paris said. "Name of Quinn.
Belonged to a drug gang called the Wreckers. On the
fringe but always looking for the main chance. Never
had the clout or the money to move into the big time."

"Just the sort of outfit Brak would buy into," Cade
said. "They'd have the local connections. He'd provide cash and the goods. You know where we can find
them?"

Paris nodded and followed Cade to the main bedroom, where Janek was guarding the pair of wounded perps.

"Any ID on these two?" Cade asked her.

"That's Keller. The other is Marchino. Slick Marchino. Local guns for hire. Handy with the violence but low on brain power. One of the perps from the chopper runs with them."

"Ryker must have picked up some info on the Wreckers tying in with Brak. He snatches Quinn and tortures what he needs to know from the guy."

Janek viewed the corpse in the bathroom. He came back shaking his head in disgust. "All this, Thomas. And for what? Explain, because I can't understand the reasoning of a mind that could do such things."

"Greed, partner. Greed and contempt for his own kind. Brak started the ball rolling back in New York. Ryker is just carrying the play. He'll do whatever he feels necessary to catch up with Brak."

Janek glanced at Paris. "I think I owe you an apology, Paris," he said. "These murderous lowlifes deserve anything that comes their way."

"Hey," the perp called Marchino said, "maybe we can cut a deal."

"Such as?" Janek asked.

"You want Ryker? I can give him to you. I know where he's gone."

Janek leaned over the man. "Help yourself by helping us," the cyborg said persuasively.

"Quinn told him there was a big meet planned for later today. Out at the Wreckers' place near Pasadena.

Brak's going to be there to put his money and know-how in the pot."

"I know where that is," Paris said.

Marchino licked his dry lips as he stared at Janek. "So do we get our deal?"

The cyborg stood upright and moved aside, turning his back on the puzzled gunman.

"Hey, our deal. We gave you the goods. What about our deal?"

Cade turned his gaze on the man. "No deals, Marchino. I'm putting you pair down for the duration. By the time you get off Mars, you won't remember where you came from."

"You lousy scumbag!" Marchino raved. "You let me..."

Cade smiled coldly. "No, pal. You did all the talking. We just listened. Nobody said anything about dealing except you."

"What about Ryker?" Keller said bitterly. "He's in just as deep."

Cade smiled. "I haven't forgotten Ryker," he said. "I'll find him. And when I do, I'll deal with him personally."

Paris crossed to the door and looked outside. "Backup's on the way," she said. "Med-cruiser coming in."

"Let's get this sorted," Cade said.

THIRTY MINUTES LATER they were on the move. The wounded perps were on the way to hospital, under Justice Department guard. Once they were fit to travel, they would be sentenced and put on board the first available flight to Mars. There wouldn't be any opportunity for appeals or deal cutting. The Justice Department had the authority to make decisions in these cases, removing society's worst offenders by the most direct means.

Paris, piloting the cruiser, took them to altitude, then placed the craft on autolock. Tracking a Justice Department air lane, the cruiser slid easily through the hazy blue sky. Paris swiveled her seat so she could face Cade and Janek.

"The Wreckers' place is in the foothills of the San Gabriel Mountains. Like I said, they're strictly small-time. But even small-time traffickers usually have fortunes. The Wreckers are an oddball bunch, representing an assortment of cultures, with plenty of outcasts and misfits from other major drug groups. Maybe they like the idea of pushing the major cartels out of the limelight. The cartels have things pretty well sewn up—they like to run things their way and they resent outsiders. The fact that the Wreckers is comprised of former members of other drug groups doesn't cut much ice with the cartels. They get pretty touchy over their pedigree."

"Like the old Mafia," Cade said. "I had to do a paper on them during my department training. They were nothing but a bunch of murdering crooks, but they swaggered around like they were something special and got real snooty if they didn't like someone."

"The Wreckers might be considered mongrels by the cartels," Paris warned, "but don't let that fool you. Mongrels or not, they're a hard bunch. You saw what Ryker had to do to Quinn to get anything out of him.

Use that as an example, Cade. Whichever way this thing goes down, you've got one hell of a fight on your hands. The Wreckers won't quit. Most of them don't even understand what the word means. And those who do will just laugh in your face.''

Janek slipped a fresh magazine into his autopistol, cocking the weapon. "Sometimes I ask myself—do I really need all this hassle? Wouldn't I be happier growing flowers or studying advanced biochemistry?''

Paris glanced at him. "Well, would you?''

Janek sighed. "Who knows? I'm damned if I do, and that's the truth.''

13

They exchanged the cruiser for an unmarked car, a classic model Cadillac Eldorado, at a local police precinct. The car was equipped with whitewall tires and was painted in a gleaming shade of pink, and the top was down.

"There's enough chrome plating on the thing to sink a space cruiser," Janek complained as he completed his tour of the vehicle. "Thomas, are you seriously suggesting we drive around in this thing?"

"Thing!" Cade said. "This is a piece of American history. Part of our culture. Like the classic Coke bottle and apple pie."

Janek sighed resignedly. "I suppose it has a certain archaic attraction."

Paris opened the passenger door and slid onto the rear seat. "Drive around California in this and no one will pay us the slightest attention."

Cade took the wheel and fired up the powerful engine. "Listen to that," he said, gripping the large steering wheel. "The sound of the American dream."

"More like one of Freddy Krueger's nightmares," Janek grumbled.

"They still showing those on TV?" Paris asked.

"On the old movie channel back in New York. They come around every month."

"I think they started losing their appeal after number thirteen."

Cade gunned the engine and took the Cadillac out into the sunlight. He rolled along the wide avenue, following Paris's directions. "This is the way to travel," he said.

"Not along Fifth Avenue it wouldn't be," Janek replied. "Not in a car this color."

"You have no romance in you, Janek."

The cyborg ignored him. He had located the on-board computer, concealed by a sliding panel under the dash. He accessed the unit and tapped into the network. Once the data bank was on-line, he keyed in some digits, then called up some information on the screen.

"This is data I picked up when we were in Kansas," he told Paris. "Part of it refers to bank account transfers. We figure Loren Brak pulled back payoffs to certain New York financiers dealing with the Outfit. He probably decided while he was snatching everything from his partners he might as well have this cash, as well."

Paris leaned forward, scanning the screen. "We can check the account numbers through the local Justice Department files," she said, giving Janek code sequences to key in. The codes provided access to the department data bank. More commands brought up fresh text.

"Interesting," Paris observed. "The bank is a fairly small operation but it carries extensive funds with a great deal of cash movement."

"Sounds like you know something we don't," Cade said.

"The reason's simple," Paris explained. "The Justice Department has had this bank under observation for the past few months because we had suspicions it was dealing in drug money—acting as a laundering broker. That's why there's so much cash flowing in and out. On the surface it looks legitimate. Apparently the bank does the payrolling for several large local companies who pay weekly in cash. Again that gives them the facility to push a lot of cash through the bank on a regular basis. Preliminary checks confirmed this. But checking via our computer network showed that there was far more in-going cash than they'd ever need."

"You haven't come up with enough evidence to move yet?" Cade asked.

Paris shook her head. "No way. These people are way ahead of us. Their lawyer is one of the best in the business. His client list includes most of the state's top criminals. He'd have us dancing on our hands within ten minutes if we didn't have one hundred-and-one-percent hard evidence. No way we could move until we had the whole damn outfit caught in the act. Know how hard that is?"

"I can just imagine," Cade said.

"One thing I can confirm," Paris continued. "We have seen one of the bank's top men in conversation with members of the Wreckers. It was a lucky break for us. We were staking out one of their safehouses and this guy turns up. Spent over an hour with them, and I'm certain they weren't negotiating a loan for a new swimming pool.''

"What about an actual connection between the Wreckers and accounts in the bank?" Janek asked.

"That's going through the data banks now," Paris explained. "The connection's there somewhere, lost in the list of phony front companies we're chasing down. We don't have anything yet."

"We've got Harmon Lyall," Janek said. "And I *know* that's Brak. We all know it.''

"Knowing and proving, Janek," Cade reminded his partner.

Janek banged his fist on the dash. "I've heard enough of this proof crap, Thomas. The three of us know who we're after, and we know they're as guilty as hell. So let's forget all this legal bull and take them out.''

"Does he often get this excited?" Paris asked.

"Every now and then," Cade answered. "I put it down to his deprived background.''

Paris chuckled. "It's interesting. I mean seeing a cyborg of Janek's advanced state displaying such human tendencies. I wonder if Dr. Landers has heard about him?''

Janek jerked around, eyes boring into Paris's face. "You know Abby?"

Paris turned away, startled by his intense stare. "Why, yes. Do you?"

"Speak her name and you talk of love," Cade said gently, unable to resist.

"Up yours, Thomas Jefferson Cade," Janek crowed. "Dr. Landers and I have an association. I'm helping her to collect data for her research into cyborg behavioral patterns."

Cade smiled. "That's what I call my association with Kate."

"That's carnal," Janek said. "Mainly to do with ripping the clothes off each other and doing *it.*"

"You said it, partner."

"Janek, I want to hear about Dr. Landers and you," Paris said. "Cade, hang a left at the next intersection, then go north."

THE HAZY OUTLINE of jagged mountain peaks rose in undulating waves beyond the low hills surrounding the Wreckers' secured estate. The compound was secluded, isolated and perfectly placed to provide the kind of security the traffickers felt they needed.

Cade drove slowly by the estate gates, noticing the armed guards just inside. As he slowed and pulled over a few hundred yards along Paris said, "Couple of cars just arrived."

Cade peered into the rearview mirror, angling it so he could pick up the image of the gate. A pair of long, black limos was waiting for the gates to open. The moment they did, the limos slid through and out of sight.

"Guy in the rear of the second car was Juan Vasco. One of the Wreckers' top men," Paris said. "Looks like our information is correct."

"So let's not waste it," Cade said, slipping the Cadillac into gear and making a fast U-turn. He throttled hard, feeling the vehicle surge forward.

"T.J.!" Janek said, pointing skyward.

Cade spotted the dark shape of a chopper over the estate. It dipped low, diving, then emitted a vivid flash followed by a plume of thick white vapor. A blurred shape erupted from the weapons pad beneath the chopper's belly. It was angled toward the ground, beyond the line of trees that blocked off the main house from the road. Seconds later the sound of an explosion reached Cade's ears.

"Ryker!" he said. "It has to be that son of a bitch!"

Cade swung around as he neared the barred gates, making the tires squeal. The heavy car slewed, almost fishtailing, but Cade hung on to the wheel and kept it under control. He kept his foot hard down, surging straight toward the gates.

"I just knew I wasn't going to like this," Janek grumbled, bracing himself.

The car struck the gates head-on, springing them open with a squeal of tortured metal. One of the two armed guards was sent flying as a swinging gate struck him.

The second guard, dodging the gates, opened up with his SMG, raking the side of the Cadillac with hot slugs.

Paris rolled out the side of the car, landing lightly, and closed in on the gun-wielding guard. As he turned to meet her attack, she launched a sweeping leg kick that struck his midsection. Driven back by the sheer force of the blow, the guard's limp form crashed against one of the stone pillars that supported the gates.

Paris retrieved the guard's abandoned SMG and searched him for extra ammo clips. Janek did the same with the first guard, then followed Paris back to the Cadillac.

"You ready now?" Cade asked. "Or would you like time to pick some flowers?"

Janek, stuffing spare ammo clips into his pocket, glanced at Paris. "All the time I get this. Nag, nag, nag. Worse than being married to the guy."

Cade floored the pedal and the Cadillac streaked along the curved drive. A thick line of trees and bushes obscured the house. More explosions rocked the area, followed by the rattle of autofire.

"Must be hell on the neighbors," Janek suggested dryly.

Armed figures burst from the dense bushes and cut across the wide lawn. Seeing the Cadillac they opened fire.

"Bail out!" Cade yelled, yanking the steering wheel hard left, bringing the Cadillac broadside on. The volley hammered at the stalled car, puncturing the steel panels.

They jumped out of the car, rolling to the ground on the blind side. Cade crouch-walked to the front of the vehicle, leaning forward to pinpoint the advancing gunners.

An autoweapon crackled harshly. Slugs clanged against the chromed front grille.

Cade pulled back.

As he did, Paris rose to her full height. Her SMG ripped out a sustained burst that raked the pair of gunners. The impact knocked them off their feet in a misty red haze.

"Clear!" Paris shouted.

They spread out, moving at a steady lope along the drive.

The attack chopper zoomed into sight over the trees, banking as it made a return run.

"He'll do it all for us," Janek said as the chopper dipped out of sight beyond the trees. "Save us the trouble if we're lucky."

Rounding a curve in the drive, they were confronted by what looked like a war zone.

The parking area in front of the house was a mess. Half a dozen cars lay in ruins. Flame and smoke gushed from the charred, blistered wrecks. Debris was scattered everywhere, and smoking craters dotted the concrete. There were a number of charred bodies sprawled around.

A flitting shadow darkened the ground. The attack chopper's rotary cannon made a deafening chatter. A relentless stream of shells chewed through everything in its path. Yelling figures scattered wildly. Some, too slow, were struck by the lashing cannon fire. Bleeding, punctured people were tossed across the concrete, some dying instantly, others screaming for help.

Cade, ducking behind a carved lawn ornament, found himself next to a lanky black guy. Wide-eyed and sweating, he stared at the Justice cop. His white suit was stained and bloody. Despite his fear, he recognized Cade as a stranger and snatched at his chrome-plated autopistol slung in a shoulder holster.

Jamming the muzzle of his Magnum under the trafficker's nose, Cade shook his head slowly. "Just isn't your day, pal."

"Who the fuck are you? You with the psycho in the chopper?"

"No way. I'm the law. Figure it as your luck changing."

Freeing plastic cuffs from a pocket, Cade ordered the trafficker to put his hands behind him. He slipped the loop over the guy's wrists and yanked it tight.

"You won't be needing this," Cade said, slipping the man's gun from its sheath and tucking it under his belt.

"What the hell you up to?"

"Just looking up an old friend."

"Like who?"

"Loren Brak."

"He what all this shit is about?"

"The guy in the chopper? Some old friends of Brak's from New York sent him. They got upset when he ran out on them with all their money. Now they want it back and Brak dead."

The black guy scowled. "You sayin' we're getting blown all to hell because Brak pissed off his partners?"

"Yeah," Cade said, enjoying the irony.

"Shit, I figured this deal had a weird smell to it all along. Brak never said anything about pullin' the sky down on us."

"So tell me where he is and I'll take him off your hands."

The black guy chuckled. "You got your nerve."

"So?"

"He's in the house. That's all I can tell you. I only just rolled in myself when all the fireworks started."

Cade twisted around the lawn ornament. The chopper had pulled away again for another sweep, leaving the area temporarily deserted. The Justice cop pushed to his feet and made a dash for the house's main entrance.

Janek's voice reached him from his right. "T.J.? I lost you."

Cade waved the cyborg over. "Brak's inside somewhere."

They ducked just inside the wide porch as someone opened up with an SMG. Slugs chewed at the brickwork, showering them with fragments. Janek, looking over his shoulder, saw the open door. He touched Cade's sleeve, and they eased inside.

Cade saw movement and turned, the Magnum rising.

A housedroid, clad in the black jacket and gray pants of a butler, lurched into view. Its hands and face were polished chrome steel. A section of the gleaming skull had been damaged, evidently by a piece of debris that had crashed through a window. The droid came to a jerky halt as it sensed Cade's presence.

"...moment, sir, and I will announce you..."

The words were repeated over and over, accompanied by repetitive movements. The damaged droid was locked in a short sequence that would encompass its entire universe until its power pack ran down.

Across the wide foyer a door swung open and armed figures burst into view, fanning out to provide protection for others following on their heels. A bunch of men clustered around the door.

"I think we've got our targets spotted," Cade said.

Janek advanced, covering Cade with his body. Some of the armed protection squad turned to force the bunched group back inside the room, while others leveled their weapons at the advancing Justice cops.

"Paris!" Janek called out.

The L.A. cop approached, her SMG laying down a line of fire that dropped one gunner. Janek's weapon joined in, taking out two more gunners.

One gunner triggered his stubby SMG, the slugs crackling against the tiled floor. He raised the muzzle at the last moment, and a trio of slugs caught Paris in the right leg, knocking her off balance for a few seconds. The cyborg twisted her slender form to come up on one knee, firing a blast of slugs into the gunner's skull. He flew backward, slamming against the wall, his shattered skull making a sticky mess.

The distraction caused by the cyborgs' combined fire gave Cade the opportunity to approach the door that had now been slammed shut. As the last gunman collapsed in a pool of his own blood, Cade slammed a shoulder against the door, bursting it open. He followed through, going into the room low and breaking to one side. He heard the explosion of gunfire and felt the impact of slugs hitting the wall above his head.

Kneeling, Cade swung the muzzle of the autopistol around. It stopped on the first of a pair of gunners who had pointed their own weapons at him.

Cade triggered quickly. A trio of .357s penetrated the guy's broad chest and he flew across the room. Cade instantly switched his aim to the second guy.

The gunner fired first. His single shot laid a slug across Cade's left side, burning a bloody line over his ribs. Then Cade responded. His aim was better. The gunner went over, arms thrown wide, blood fanning out across his shirt from the heart shot.

Behind the retreating traffickers Cade saw wide glass doors open to the rear of the house, and beyond, a wide expanse of lawn.

Somewhere near the doors other gunmen were trying to get a clear shot at Cade. He moved deeper into the room, dodging behind a large executive-style desk.

One gunner stepped clear of the group and fired his autoweapon. Slugs bored into the polished desktop, filling the air with splinters. Cade tipped the heavy piece of furniture on its side, keeping low as more slugs thudded into the thick wood. He dragged himself to the edge of the desk and rolled around, his gun hand ahead of him. He picked up the figure of the gunner, leaned out and triggered hard and fast.

The guy bounced as slugs pierced his upper chest, spinning him off his feet. He hit the floor cursing wildly but still gripping his SMG. Struggling to sit, he turned the gun on Cade's partially exposed figure. Cade shot again, planting a slug directly between the guy's wide, angry eyes. The gunner flopped over on his back, heels drumming in protest against the plush carpet.

Pulling back into cover, Cade ejected the spent magazine and fumbled for a fresh one. His fingers brushed against his side, coming away sticky with blood. He ignored the sight and the nagging pain and jammed a fresh magazine into the weapon.

A shadow brushed across the upturned desk. Cade twisted around to see a gaudily dressed trafficker lunge with a slim-bladed switchblade.

Cade ducked as the keen blade sliced the air and scarred the desktop. The Justice cop swept his right leg around in a half circle, catching the guy behind the ankles and knocking his feet from under him. The trafficker crashed against the desk, grunting as the breath was slammed from his lungs. He made a blind slash with the knife, almost catching Cade's arm.

In the heat of the moment the trafficker lunged upright, as though forgetting Cade's gun. He thrust the tip of the switchblade at Cade's face. Cade eased back, then whacked the butt of the Magnum against the guy's nose. Blood spurted in thick gouts from his nostrils. He clapped one hand to his nose, bellowing with wild rage. He swung his knife arm again but missed, and the force turned him halfway around. Cade jammed the muzzle of the Magnum against his opponent's left side and pulled the trigger. The slug blew out the other side, taking ribs and flesh with it. The trafficker went down in a loose heap.

"You going to play about all day?" Janek called as he and Paris burst through the door.

Ignoring his partner's jibe, Cade ran for the open glass doors. The way was clear now. The traffickers and their protectors had taken advantage of Cade's delay and had scattered.

As Janek appeared a burst of autofire shattered the glass door. He dropped to one knee, lifted his SMG and returned fire. The gunman was caught square in the chest and went down in the middle of a smooth, expansive lawn.

"You see Brak?" Cade asked.

"There," Paris said.

Cade followed her pointing finger.

Loren Brak, flanked by a trio of men, was closing in on a black truck. Other vehicles were parked on a small paved area beside the house.

"Not again," Cade muttered. "He ran out on me too many times."

He ran parallel with the back of the house, using lawn ornaments and shrubbery as cover.

Janek pounded after him, laying down shots to dissuade the remaining gunners from interfering.

There was a moment when Paris thought of joining them, but her attention was drawn by the attack chopper as it swung across the rear lawn, raking everyone in sight with the rotary cannon. Gouts of earth spouted up as shells pounded the ground. Easy targets, the scattering traffickers went down like grass beneath a windstorm.

Reloading her SMG, Paris watched the chopper come in for a landing. The hatches slid open and disgorged a quartet of armed figures. The cyborg recognized Ryker but none of the others, although she knew their profession. They were hired guns, men who earned their living by the killing trade.

Glancing at Janek's retreating figure, Paris realized
that the New York cops had their hands full going after Loren Brak. They didn't need Ryker on their tails
right now.

She ran forward, SMG held ready. "Justice marshal. You're under arrest, Ryker. I want those hands up
high where I can see them."

A couple of the hired guns hesitated. Ryker didn't
even break his stride. Paris even saw him grin. She reminded herself that this was the man who had insti-
gated the death of Wexler, her partner.

She triggered, taking out one of the gunners. She
aimed the follow-up volley at the chopper. The slugs
cored through the hatch vent cover and tore into the
electronic control panels, efficiently disabling the machine.

Ryker's other gunners returned fire. They were good,
too. Worthy of their pay, Paris thought as her titanium-steel flexi-coat absorbed the impact of the autofire. The force pushed her to her knees. Paris's clothing
shredded, and her synthetic skin split to expose the
gleaming steel beneath.

"It's a cybo!" one of the gunners yelled a second
before Paris laid a trio of slugs through his skull.

"You can't stop those fuckers," another said.

"Can't you?" Ryker said.

For a microsecond his eyes locked with Paris's.

His gun hand came up, the big autopistol lining up
rock steady, and Paris read deep into his mind.

The pistol fired.

Once.

And just before the slug cored in through Paris's right eyepiece, she knew the truth about Ryker.

But by then it was too late.

Her electronic mind blew apart in a blinding flash.

For Paris the world closed down permanently.

14

Janek was never sure afterward why he looked back over his shoulder.

But he retained the memory of what he saw.

In the second he looked back, Ryker triggered the single shot that ended Paris's existence. The female cyborg was driven to the ground by the powerful slug that ripped into her skull and destroyed her brain.

Janek wanted to turn and go after Ryker. But his loyalty was to Cade, and nothing could have drawn him from that.

He followed his partner, conscious of the probability of Brak's slipping through their fingers again.

ACROSS THE LAWN Ryker turned and watched the line of pursuit, recognizing the figures in the distance.

His prime objective was Loren Brak. And if the pair of Justice cops got in his way, they would also be removed. He gestured to his remaining accomplices, and they moved to join the chase.

Cade felt a burning ache across his side. He knew he was losing blood from the bullet crease and that loss would be increased due to his exertions. But there was no stopping now. No way was he quitting.

He stumbled, scraping against the side of the house. The rough wall gouged his flesh. Cade shoved himself upright, away from the wall, and kept on running.

Brak had reached the truck. One of his gunners had slipped behind the wheel, kicking the powerful engine to life.

The gunner shielding Brak cut loose with his high-power combat rifle, pumping shot after shot in Cade's direction. The third gunner helped Brak into the truck.

Janek tracked the guy with his SMG. The burst he fired was short, the autoweapon locking on an empty magazine. Shaking his head in frustration, the cybo dragged his handgun free and used that instead.

The gunner with the rifle was the last to climb into the truck as it lurched into motion. Janek's shots clipped the rear fender. Doors were still flapping as the vehicle burned rubber across the concrete, heading around the house toward the open drive beyond.

Both Cade and Janek laid concentrated fire at the escaping truck. Slugs sparked off the vehicle's toughened bodywork and blew out the rear screen.

Cade cut across the concrete, reaching a gleaming black Ford Cobra-2. The gull-wing doors sprang open as he stroked the touchpad. Leaning inside, he saw that the key was in the ignition. He dropped into the driver's contoured leather seat. As he fired up the turbo-boosted engine, Janek slid into the passenger seat. Cade slammed the car into gear and popped the clutch. The wide tires squealed in protest. Cade spun the wheel, taking the sleek roadster in pursuit of the truck.

"On his tail, T.J.," Janek said. "Not up his ass."

"Watch me, partner."

Janek locked the safety belt as the gull-wing doors sealed. He shook his head in disbelief as Cade took the Ford along the drive, out through the gates and into a slithering turn.

The truck was already way along the road, dwindling rapidly as it picked up speed.

The chase took them through the hilly country bordering the San Gabriel foothills.

"Where the hell is he going?" Janek asked. "Is he just running scared, or has he got a place to go?"

Cade shrugged. "Maybe he arranged a backup plan to save himself if things went sour here in L.A. But I really don't know. Brak's no fool. If he has to run, he'll cut his losses and do it. He must have known that play was on the cards. You don't ice your partners, grab the loot and run, without somebody getting slightly pissed off. He has to have a place somewhere where he can vanish and lie low until the heat eases off. He can afford it with all the cash he took. Plus the accounts he transferred from New York. And he still has the formula for Thunder Crystals. So he isn't going to be strapped for cash."

"He stays out of the light for a few months, then surfaces and starts over."

"Wise move."

"Only if we let him get away with it, T.J."

"No way, partner. Not with three Justice cops dead in New York and Wexler here in L.A."

"Paris is finished, too. I saw her take a headshot back at the house."

"Then there's no damn way he's walking free."

The truck hung a sharp right. Cade almost overshot and had to stand on the brake to bring the car around in a groaning slide. He floored the pedal, feeling the power surge, hoping to regain some ground between them and the distant truck.

"No way we can bring in backup on this one," Janek observed. "This is going to be down to us, Thomas."

"Tell me something I don't know."

Janek leaned back in his seat, deciding silence was the order of the day—for the short term at least.

His gaze wandered to the rearview mirror, picking up the silver Chrysler a few hundred yards back. His interest was aroused when he recognized the car. It had been parked with the others at the rear of the traffickers' house.

Janek allowed himself a thin smile. He knew without actually seeing the man who it was behind the wheel.

Ryker!

Someone else who refused to quit.

UP AHEAD THE TRUCK hit a sharp curve, and the rear end slid a little. Bouncing along the grass, the vehicle raised a cloud dust that whipped back to obscure Cade's vision for a few seconds.

He swore under his breath, dropping his own speed and falling back.

As the dust cleared, he spotted the truck vanishing over the crest of a rise. Cade stamped on the gas pedal, and the Ford went up the slope with the slickness of a shuttle craft leaving a launching ramp. The wheels left the ground as it cleared the crest, bottoming out as it came back down to earth.

"Thomas, what the fuck are you trying to do?" Janek yelled, completely losing his usual restraint.

"Relax," Cade said, grinning.

"*Relax!* T.J., you're a menace when you get behind a wheel."

"Doing the job, partner, that's all."

"So's Ryker," Janek said evenly.

"Say what?"

"Ryker. He's on our tail."

Cade checked the mirror. "Hell! Why didn't you tell me?"

"I just did."

"Great timing, partner."

Janek checked his weapons. "Get me in range, and I'll try and take out one of their tires," the cyborg suggested.

Cade pumped more gas to the engine. He felt it leap forward and realized the vehicle-to-vehicle gap was closing.

They were pushing higher into the hills now. There wasn't much traffic around. The narrow highway cut a tortuous path around the rolling slopes. Cade swung back and forth, trying to get alongside the truck, but the driver behind the wheel kept him at bay by countering Cade's moves.

"Smart son of a bitch."

"Long straight coming up," Janek said. "Go for it."

Cade leaned on the pedal, bringing them close up to the truck's rear.

Cocking the SMG, Janek powered his window down and leaned out.

"Now, T.J.!"

Cade swung around the truck's rear, catching the driver out and holding the Ford alongside.

Janek leaned farther out, aiming the SMG at the truck's rear wheel. He loosed off a short burst into the tire, shredding the thick rubber.

"Back off!" he yelled to Cade, pulling back into the car.

Cade slackened off the gas pedal, touching the brake and allowing the Ford to drop back.

The truck sank onto the rim of the blown tire. A thick stream of orange sparks leaped up from the road. The heavy vehicle began to slew from side to side as the driver fought the wheel.

"Ryker coming up!" Janek yelled.

Cade glanced in the rearview mirror and saw the silver Chrysler looming large. His drop in speed had closed the gap, bringing Ryker closer than anticipated.

The cars made contact, metal and plastic burning against each other. Bits flew into the air.

Cade felt the car shudder. He touched the gas pedal, pulling ahead again, but he was forced to brake again almost immediately as he saw the fishtailing truck directly ahead.

"Damn!"

They were trapped between the truck and Ryker's Chrysler, with nowhere to go. A high bank lay on the right and a steep slope on the left.

Janek twisted around and climbed into the rear seat. Clenching his fist, he punched out the rear window

Poking the SMG through the gap, the cyborg sprayed the pursuing vehicle, caving in the windshield. The Chrysler dropped back, swerving violently, and gouged the earthy bank as it slowed in a series of jerky bumps.

Touching the brake again, Cade eased away from the truck. The driver appeared to have regained some control despite the burst tire. He pulled it around a sharp curve, compensating for the drift, and as the road straightened, poured on the power.

A signboard flashed by, too quickly for Cade to read.

"You catch that?" he asked over his shoulder.

"Of course, T.J., it's my advantage over you. Better vision. Faster reflexes."

"And I have a lower boredom level, so give," Cade snapped.

"Half mile ahead there's a turning for a feeder road. It leads to a small landing field."

"Damn it, I knew he wasn't just running blind."

"Meaning?"

"Brak's going to break for that field. He's got a craft of some kind waiting there for him. Cruiser maybe. Strato-jumper. Anything to get him out of here so he can vanish."

"Sounds logical."

"Logic, my ass. The guy's a survivor, Janek. I'll bet my next salary check he had this arranged months ago. While he was setting up his deals. Brak had to know he'd catch hell when this broke, so he took out insurance."

The hard-running truck turned onto the feeder road, trailing smoke and sparks. It bumped and lurched along the narrow strip, with Cade in close pursuit.

"There's somebody at the tailgate door," Janek warned.

Cade saw the tailgate door flip open. It was pulled upward by the slipstream from the speeding vehicle. A figure was hunched in the shadow of the passenger compartment. Janek leaned over the seat, focusing on the guy's activities.

"Grenade!" he yelled.

The small, spherical object flew from the truck, hit the road and bounced. It seemed to be coming directly at the windshield. Cade yanked hard on the wheel, swinging away.

There was a bright flash, and the grenade exploded with a sharp crash. The windows along the left side were blown in, showering the interior with glass particles. Cade felt the sharp bite of glass sting his face.

From behind he heard Janek being thrown across the rear seat, crashing against the interior panel.

"You okay?" he called over his shoulder.

For a moment Janek didn't speak. Then he gave a low croaking sound. After a few seconds his voice returned to normal. "As you would say, T.J., the son of a bitch got me."

Janek's left arm slid over the seat. His jacket and shirt had been blown off his arm, and his syntho-flesh was shredded, exposing his titanium-steel limb.

"Keep your eye on that sucker," Janek said.

He retrieved his SMG and swung it out the window, leaning out precariously. Cade eased over to the side of the road, giving Janek the target acquisition space he needed.

"Bastard's got another," Cade said.

Janek raised the SMG, aiming and triggering a burst that punctured the grenade thrower's chest. The guy slumped, then toppled over the lower tailgate, flopping onto the road. Cade had no time to avoid him. The Ford bounced over the body, dragging it for a few yards. Seconds after they rolled clear, the grenade exploded, throwing dirt and stone chips over the car's rear.

The truck swerved through the open gates of the field. A security droid stepped out, waving its arms as it tried to flag the vehicle down. The front of the truck struck the droid and sent it flying, and the truck cut across the landing field's concrete apron.

Checking the way ahead, Cade pushed the Ford in pursuit. The truck seemed to be heading for a sleek blue-and-scarlet strato-jumper parked in the corner of the small airfield.

As Cade rolled through the gates, he picked up the shape of Ryker's Chrysler behind him, coming up fast.

The strato-jumper was a twenty-five-foot craft. One of the new breed of flyers designed for swift, long-distance travel, it was shaped like a sleek, narrow wedge with a needle nose. Strato-jumpers operated by using high-power rocket engines that pushed them into the stratosphere, where they cruised before reentering and gliding down to computer-tracked landing coordinates.

"That jumper is ready to go," Janek said.

Pale vapor was drifting from the craft's exhaust ports, showing that the powerful engines had been put on warm-up.

"Brak must have called ahead," Cade grumbled, trying to up their speed. "He doesn't waste a damn minute."

The limping truck skidded as it reached the strato-jumper. Before it came to rest, the doors sprang open. Loren Brak, carrying a pair of lightweight alloy cases, ran for the craft's open hatch. One of his gunners followed, protecting Brak's rear, while the remaining gunner leaned across the truck's hood and opened up with an autorifle. The powerful combat weapon cracked viciously, laying a steady volley of shots into the Ford.

"Son of a bitch!" Cade yelled. He swung the Ford around and aimed it at the truck. It struck head-on, shoving the truck across the concrete and knocking the gunner off his feet.

"Get Brak," Cade said, struggling to open his jammed door. "I'll handle Ryker."

Janek sprang out, his legs moving in a blur as he ran for the strato-jumper.

The craft was already moving on its launch dolly as the automatic control eased it toward the runway strip.

Brak and his protector had vanished inside, and the hatch was starting to close.

Janek didn't hesitate.

He poured on the power, angling his line of travel as he closed in on the strato-jumper.

Cade, kicking open his jammed door, emerged in time to see his cyborg partner take a flying leap through the hatch before it closed.

Moments later the strato-jumper locked onto the runway strip. There was a deep-seated roar from the rocket engines. A plume of flame and smoke erupted from the exhaust ports. The jumper gathered itself then vanished along the strip, picking up speed with a terrifying roar. It parted company with the launch dolly and burned its way toward the stratosphere, vanishing from sight in the clear blue California sky.

15

Janek lost his grip on the SMG as he went through the hatchway. There wasn't a thing he could do about it. He hit the compartment floor, tucking his shoulder in and rolling. His forward momentum carried him across the compartment, and he crashed against the padded bulkhead. He quickly scrambled to his feet.

He'd expected armed response from Brak and his gunner, possibly more if the drug trafficker had extra heavies inside the strato-jumper.

He hadn't expected an android protector.

As Janek climbed to his feet, he saw something move to his left. Turning that way, he was met by a hard backhand across the side of his head. The blow sent him reeling. Janek felt his circuits fade for a moment. He picked up movement again. This time he ducked under the slashing arm of his attacker.

He lunged for his opponent. The moment he came up against the dull black casing, he realized this was no human bodyguard. Brak had hired a minder droid. The classification for the model was personal-protection droid and, correctly programmed, they were ideal bodyguards. But many illegal models had been created, their internal program circuits altered. The droids had become muscle for the likes of Brak, men who wanted more than a droid willing to protect. These droids would kill to order and maim as a matter of course. They were tough, resilient and brutal.

Janek dug his feet hard against the compartment deck and shoved, driving the droid off balance. He heard the droid's grunt of surprise. It hadn't expected a cyborg adversary. Given a few moments, it would adjust its defensive mode to take into account the fact it was dealing with something more than a weak human.

Janek didn't intend giving the droid that chance. He jammed the heel of his right hand under the droid's broad jaw and shoved hard. The droid gave a squawk as its neck reached the extreme limit of flexibility. Janek kept pushing. He heard the soft snap of the droid's central circuit cord, which was embedded in the tubular coil that ran from neck to waist—the droid's "spine." The droid immediately went limp.

Shoving the robot aside, Janek glanced around the compartment. He wasn't alone. Brak had vanished through the hatch that led to the control cabin. Between Janek and the trafficker was Brak's sole surviving protector, armed and obviously ready to use his weapon.

The strato-jumper, already on the move as Janek had made his entrance, gave a powerful surge. Pressure built up suddenly as the craft leaped along the runway strip. Janek was slammed back against the bulkhead. He watched the gunner stumble, unable to cope with the incredible acceleration. He should have been strapped into one of the launch couches. As the stumbling figure slid toward him across the compartment, Janek simply waited.

The protector tried to lift his weapon but couldn't overcome the pressure that was adding to his body weight.

Janek had no problems. He simply pumped up his servo circuit, reaching out with a clenched fist. It slammed across the oncoming man's jaw with un- yielding force, snapping his head back, blood spray- ing in thick droplets from the crushed lips. The gunner released his weapon, which Janek grabbed, and slid into the bulkhead. From there the gunner rolled to the floor, ending up as an inert bundle.

Janek pressed himself against the bulkhead until the strato-jumper leveled out at cruising altitude. Speed dropped and the pressure lessened.

Unloading the combat rifle and pocketing the mag- azine, he crossed the compartment and opened the hatch to the control cabin.

"You handle that—" Loren Brak began.

Then he realized that the figure coming in through the hatch wasn't his protector.

"You!" Brak yelled, grabbing for the autopistol holstered under his shoulder. "Do I have to get rid of you myself?"

The dark-haired pilot, the only other person in the control cabin, rounded on Brak. "Not in here! Not a frigging gun, for Christ's sake."

Brak ignored him. The trafficker's grand plan had been thwarted right from the moment Cade and Janek were assigned to the investigation. They had followed him across the country, from east to west, breaking up his organization. Nothing seemed to stop them. Like a pair of avenging angels, Cade and Janek had trailed him all the way. Even now one had followed him on board the strato-jumper.

The autopistol angled up, the muzzle lining up on Janek's face, wavering between his eyes. There was a split second before Brak made the unconscious decision to go for the cyborg's right eyepiece.

That hesitation was Janek's chance—and he took it without a second thought.

Janek's arm swung up, striking Brak's gun hand. The autopistol swung off Janek, and the trafficker's finger jerked back against the trigger as he lost control of his reflexes.

The roar of the heavy-caliber pistol filled the cabin. The slug erupted from the muzzle, hitting the pilot in the back of the neck at close range. It cored through his throat in a gory mush, then deflected against the edge of the control panel.

Cursing wildly, Loren Brak attempted to hit Janek with his gun hand. Janek swayed to one side, barely noticing the gun barrel as it caught the side of his face, splitting the syntho-flesh. He slipped a hand under Brak's gun arm, closed his other over the trafficker's wrist, lifting and pulling. Brak was raised on his toes as the cybo piled on the pressure.

The pistol slipped from numb fingers, clattering to the deck. Janek kicked it aside, then swung Brak around, slamming him face first against the bulkhead. Brak let out a strangled groan, blood streaming from his crushed nose and split lips.

"You bastard. That hurt."

"It was meant to," Janek said with feeling.

Despite his injury, Brak stared at the cyborg. "Meant to? You cybos ain't supposed to get personal."

Janek registered the trafficker's words and realized he was right.

Cyborgs were supposed to be above human frailties such as rage and wanting revenge.

"Damned if you're not correct," Janek said, a trace of surprise in his tone.

And then he hit Brak again, spinning the trafficker across the cabin and dumping him on the deck.

Janek dragged the dead pilot out of the way, hoping to bring the straying strato-jumper back under control. He slid into the seat, punching the button that jettisoned the rocket pod. As it fell clear, leaving the jumper without power, he tapped into the on-board computer, quickly laying down coordinates for a controlled-glide landing. He felt the craft start to tumble, his powerful fingers working the manual controls.

The strato-jumper's glide fins slid out from the main fuselage, locking into place. Janek became aware of the bumpiness subsiding. He tested the control sensitivity and found it expanding. He peered through the view canopy at the terrain below.

Checking the monitor, Janek identified the landing strip. He eased the controls to bring the craft around. On-screen text detailed distance and height, the computer quickly giving him necessary data for a reasonably safe landing. According to the results, it was going to be a short landing, with no room for error.

"I'll make it," Janek said out loud. "I always knew I would."

He saw the strip coming up, and the sight made him wonder how Cade was getting on with Ryker.

CADE DROPPED to the ground, rolling beneath the stalled truck. Emerging on the far side, he snatched up the combat rifle dropped by the dead gunner. Ignoring the bloody mush that had been the guy's chest, Cade located a couple of spare mags for the weapon and jammed them inside his jacket.

He heard the screech of tires as the Chrysler slid to a stop. Peering under the truck, Cade saw feet hit the ground as Ryker and two men piled out.

Making certain the high-powered rifle was cocked, Cade eased to the rear corner of the truck. He took a quick look to pinpoint the position of Ryker and his partners.

One of the hired guns stepped into view. Cade raised the rifle, aimed and fired in one easy movement. The slug took the gunner in the chest, and he fell back against the car's hood. Cade laid a second shot into him for good measure.

Moving to the front of the truck, Cade heard rapid footsteps as Ryker and the remaining gunner took cover.

Lying flat, Cade scanned the area around the Chrysler. He spotted a pair of feet at the rear of the vehicle. Bringing the rifle to his shoulder, he flipped the fire selector to 3-round bursts. He triggered, aiming at the rear of the Chrysler. The slugs punched ragged holes in the bodywork, and some reached the concealed gunner. Cade heard a grunt of pain, then the gunner broke from cover, firing indiscriminately at Cade's position.

The moment he had a clear shot, Cade emptied the rifle's magazine. The gunner's body jerked and twitched as the 3-round bursts cored into his flesh.

Propelled by the impact, the dying man stumbled awkwardly, falling.

Cade ejected the spent magazine, snapped in a fresh one. With the weapon cocked and ready he pressed against the cold metal of the truck, ears straining to pick up any sound that might pinpoint Ryker's position.

What he did hear was the roar of an engine. Tires bit into the earth, scattering debris as Ryker reversed, then knocked the gear into forward. The car lurched toward the rear of the truck, ramming it. The impact shoved it forward a couple of feet, knocking Cade away from the side.

Cade rolled clear and came to his feet, the rifle held at hip level. He could see Ryker's wildly grinning face behind the starred windshield of the Chrysler. Cade shot into the windshield, and Ryker jerked back, ramming the gas pedal to pull the Chrysler back and forth, using it like a battering ram. He caught the back corner of the truck, pushing the vehicle around. Cade took a headlong dive to stay out of the way. He crashed to the ground on his shoulder, bruising it badly. Aware of the engine's manic roar, he rolled frantically. Coming over on his back, he saw the vehicle bearing down on him.

He let out a yell as he dug his heels into the earth to gain some leverage and shove himself away from the churning wheels. He only just made it. Peppering him with dirt and dust, the Chrysler rocked by with inches to spare. The car shot ahead, braked savagely, then reversed, its tires throwing up acrid smoke as Ryker jammed the pedal to the floor, the rear end fishtailing.

Cade sat upright, locking the rifle against his hip. He pumped shot after shot into the car's rear section, blowing the tires to shreds and puncturing the gas tank.

At the last moment he kicked off to the side, feeling the fender brush his shoulder. The impact did more to fuel Cade's anger than anything else.

Ryker's snarling features, streaked with blood, showed as a quick blur as the Chrysler slid by.

Up on one knee, Cade blasted the rifle through the side window. Ryker jerked and rolled, still gripping the wheel. But the engine stalled and the car humped to a dead stop.

Pumping from the ruptured tank, raw fuel was pooling under the car's rear. Cade cut around the Chrysler, reaching into his pocket for the disposable lighter he carried for his cigars. His thumb flicked the button, and a thin tongue of flame shot out. Vapor ignited with a soft whoosh, spreading quickly under the car and to the wide pool on the ground.

As he ran, Cade heard the grinding of the starter as Ryker made an attempt to restart the Chrysler.

There was a deep roar as the flames reached the tank and it blew, flame boiling out in all directions. Cade felt the shock wave reach out and slam him to the ground, the heat of the fireball scorching the back of his jacket.

Up on his feet again, Cade turned to shield his face from the heat. Debris rattled to the ground around him. A thick pall of smoke hung over the blazing vehicle.

Cade was about to turn away when he heard the groan of buckling metal. The driver's door, its paint peeling under the heat, slowly swung open on protesting hinges.

From the fire-scorched front of the Chrysler a figure half climbed, half stumbled out. It rose to its full height, turning to Cade.

The Justice cop found himself face-to-face with a living nightmare.

It was Ryker, or what was left of him.

Most of his clothing had gone, as had the major part of his flesh. His face, blistered and peeling, was still recognizable, the shriveling flesh shelling off like fish scales. Fluid oozed from the pores. A bright halo of fire encircled his skull as his hair burned away. Where the flesh had parted from the body, Cade could see the gleam of bright metal, sinews and muscle that were fine strands of platinum wire and silicone pads.

Ryker stepped away from the burning wreck, his naked feet leaving bloody prints. His right hand, gripping the door for support, shed strips of fatty tissue as he pulled it free.

He advanced slowly, his agony showing in the eyes glaring defiantly from the bony skull.

Cade gripped the combat rifle with sweaty hands. Whatever he might have expected to see, this vision of hell was not it.

Ryker, part man, part machine, was a result of the out-and-out commercial area of bionics that persisted despite the ban years earlier. At isolated clinics biosurgeons took willing human patients and transformed them into the artfully blended hybrids known as biofreaks.

Anything was possible, from a simple limb replacement to a full body transplant. All it took was one of the maverick doctors and a client with plenty of money. It was as easy as that.

The assassin known as Ryker had opted for the full transplant. His head was his own, as were the organs encased within a thin steel torso. Everything else was the creation of the biosurgeon who had carved up Ryker's living flesh and installed the limbs of titanium, silicone and platinum wire. Over all this, organic outer flesh had grown, complete with active veins and circulating blood fed by the still-pumping heart. It had created the most formidable hitman ever. The swift responses of the intricate bionics, merged with a natural brain and internal organs, had produced a being of extreme power and cunning.

But even Ryker was fallible. Despite his above-human reaction time and superb response capabilities, even he had found it impossible to escape the awesome speed and power of man's most unforgiving adversary—fire. Caught in the raging maelstrom, he had been reduced to a near-skeletal form.

"So it's you," Ryker rasped, the words delivered in a voice that was one step from the grave. Superheated air had ravaged his vocal cords, leaving him with little more than a hoarse whisper. He stumbled over the words, forming them with great difficulty and forcing them through shrunken, bleeding, black lips. "But it isn't over until I rip out your heart!"

Ryker summoned his remaining strength and lunged forward, his titanium-reinforced hands reaching for Cade. The unreasoning wildness in his staring eyes might have unnerved a lesser man.

"You were wrong there, pal," Cade said. "It's over—and I mean *now!*"

His hands activated the combat rifle, leveling it at the monstrous figure bearing down on him.

He pumped shot after shot into Ryker's naked skull until it burst apart, flesh and bone disintegrating in a burst of pulpy red and gray. Ryker let out a final howl of pure rage and agony, then crashed to the ground a couple of feet from Cade.

The massive figure thrashed in final convulsions, slowing imperceptibly until it gave a last shudder and became still, blood seeping from the shattered head into the thirsty earth.

Cade threw aside the rifle. He turned away and crossed to the wrecked truck. Leaning against it, he pulled a crumpled cigar from his pocket and put it in his mouth. Then he recalled that he'd lost his lighter after setting off the gas leaking from Ryker's car. He threw the cigar aside. He was starting to ache, and he could feel blood streaming down the side of his face from a bad scrape.

From a distance came the sound of vehicles crossing the field from the landing strip's control tower. It wouldn't be long before a police cruiser would come howling up. At that moment Cade couldn't have cared less.

He was wondering where Janek was.

The strato-jumper appeared then, swooping in from the empty sky, descending at a steep angle.

Too steep, Cade realized as he watched it drop. The jumper hit the end of the strip and bounced wildly, almost overturning. Then it settled, veering as it sped along the strip, metal scraping the concrete and raising great sparks. Chunks of metal broke free. With a loud grating sound the strato-jumper made a final lurch, then skidded off the strip, ploughing up earth and grass in a great swath. One fin snapped off as the jumper rolled and spun in a wide arc before coming to rest.

Cade moved to where the strato-jumper lay. Sparks crackled and popped from severed cables exposed by ripped-off panels in the outer skin. As he neared the craft, the hatch slid open with a groan of damaged servos.

Janek's battered figure appeared in the opening. The cyborg grinned when he took in Cade's equally shabby appearance.

"You look like hell," Janek observed. "I take it you managed to deal with Ryker?"

"It was a struggle without you, but I managed."

"I brought you something back," Janek said brightly.

He reached down and hauled a limp figure into view. With a heave of his arm the cyborg dumped Loren Brak on the ground at Cade's feet.

"This is the guy who started all this. So we can finish it with him, as well."

"Let's get the cuffs on him before he does another runner on us."

Janek secured Brak's hands behind his back, then cuffed the trafficker's ankles. "Beat that, sucker," he said cheerfully.

Returning to the strato-jumper, Janek vanished inside. When he climbed out a few minutes later, Cade was in conversation with a uniformed California highway patrol officer. Loren Brak, bloody and silent, was in the rear of the patrol car, a sleek black-and-white FireCruiser.

Close by were an assortment of vehicles, with interested spectators being kept back by a couple of android cops. A med-cruiser came drifting silently over the field.

Janek had a couple of aluminum cases in his hands. He dropped them beside Cade.

"And this is what it was all about, T.J. Cash. Drug formula. Enough Thunder Crystals to feed a city for six months."

"Anything else in there?"

Janek nodded. "Every name you ever wanted to hear. The information in here will shut down a dozen operations between here and New York."

"What about our city money men?"

Janek nodded. "Confirmation of the names we picked up. Locations. Dates. Amounts paid. Almost makes it too easy for us."

"I could use a little easy time, partner," Cade said. "The sooner we get back to New York, the better I'll feel. Then we can go and shut down these money men."

Janek nodded his approval. "That'll do for me, T.J.," he said.

And he meant it.

EPILOGUE

New York City

"Can't you make better time than this?" Randolph asked impatiently. Agitated and nervous, he was sweating profusely, despite the fact that it was raining heavily outside the motionless limousine.

The vehicle, like many others, was stalled on the crowded approach to the Holland Tunnel, locked in a mass of cars on a late afternoon in a torrential downpour from a darkening sky.

Beside Randolph on the limo's spacious rear seat sat Mennard, the bodyguard he had hired a week or so back. The man was large and solid, seemingly unaffected by any situation. As Randolph posed the question, Mennard leaned forward to peer through the rain-streaked windshield.

"Not a great deal we can do, Mr. Randolph," he said evenly. "Traffic looks pretty well locked in."

"Damn!"

Randolph slumped back in the plush seat. For once he was unable to derive his usual pleasure from the limo's luxurious surroundings. In better times he reveled in the vehicle's customized decadence. Right now it was taking on the ambience of a costly jail cell.

Mennard tapped the driver on the shoulder, leaning close to pass a message to the man.

"What?" Randolph asked, unsettled by the whispered conversation. "Mennard?"

"Relax, Mr. Randolph," the bodyguard said. "It's all taken care of. I've got it fixed to get you out of here."

The financier stared out through the limo's tinted window. The traffic lanes on either side were choked with idling vehicles. The lines stretched into the distance both ahead and behind. As far as Randolph could see, there was no way out.

"Mennard, I don't wish to appear negative, but how the hell do we get out of this mess?" Randolph indicated the traffic snarl. "You've seen what's out there?"

"Easy to see you're not a religious man, Mr. Randolph," Mennard said, smiling thinly.

Randolph scowled, causing Mennard to smile even more.

"No faith," the bodyguard explained. "You have no faith."

Randolph allowed himself a dry chuckle. "In what? Miracles? Is that what you mean? Fucking miracles dropping down from the sky?"

"Yes, sir," Mennard replied. "That's exactly what I mean."

Puzzled, Randolph watched as the bodyguard opened his door and stepped into the downpour. The financier stared at the man, convinced he was going crazy. He was about to voice his opinion when Mennard stuck his head back inside. Rainwater was dripping from his face, and his expensive suit was sodden.

"Shall we get our asses into gear, Mr. Randolph, sir?" he said respectfully.

Sliding his plump form along the leather seat, Randolph peered out into the rain and saw a sleek executive air cruiser hovering just above the level of the limo's roofline. An alloy ladder had been extended to within a foot of the ground.

"What's this?" Randolph asked as he pushed himself out of the limo. The drenching rain went unnoticed as Randolph reached for the ladder and freedom.

"My backup," Mennard said. "A precaution against anything going wrong. I had a feeling we might hit heavy traffic, this being a weekend."

"Which is why I chose to leave," Randolph insisted as he climbed the ladder. "The best time to slip away from under the noses of those damn Justice cops."

He hauled himself up the ladder, the effort winding him. His fingers ached as he gripped the rungs. The discomfort was worth it, he decided, because he *had* fooled the bastard called T. J. Cade.

And that was worth a lot in Randolph's book.

During the past few days Cade had been busy hauling in Randolph's associates, his partners in crime. And while that had been happening, Randolph, always a man who looked to the future, had put into operation his own survival plan.

One of his steps had been to hire a personal chauffeur and bodyguard. Mennard had been paid for by Randolph alone, and the investment was already paying off, because the others were behind bars while he was free.

Once he was on board the cruiser, the rest of his trip to the Newark Air and Shuttle Port would be rapidly completed. If he was able to make his connection and get on the strato-jumper, he could be halfway around the world before the cops found out. He had friends abroad and he had already transferred his assets, so there was no reason for him to stay in New York.

Randolph, sweating even more than before and soaked through from the rain, heaved himself through the open hatch and felt a firm hand grasp his arm.

"Let me give you a hand, Mr. Randolph."

Someone's strong fingers gripped him. A moment later he was hauled bodily into the cruiser and the hatch was closed with a solid thump.

"Wait," Randolph protested. "We forgot Mennard."

"We didn't forget him, Randolph. He'll have company by now. From the NYPD."

Randolph lifted his dripping head and stared at the speaker.

He found himself face-to-face with Janek. The cyborg had an amused smile on his lips as he studied the financier's incredulous expression.

"T.J., I think you win your bet," he said.

"What did I tell you?" Cade acknowledged. He appeared from a corner of the cabin. "Hell of a day, Randolph."

The financier stared at the Justice cop. "Mennard?" he said.

Janek shook his head. "He's as dumb as you, Randolph. We've been watching him for days. Led us right to this cruiser and you."

Randolph climbed to his feet, glancing from the cyborg to Cade. Beyond Cade the financier could see the lights of the city shimmering through the falling rain, glittering brightly against the dullness of the day. They seemed to mock him, saying, here we are, Randolph.

So close but getting farther away with each passing second.

Realization dawned on Randolph that everything was slipping away from his grasp. He had not escaped after all. On the contrary, he had walked right into Cade's hands. The Justice cop had simply played his waiting game and Randolph had appeared on cue.

So much for his clever plans. He had been fooling himself all along, believing he was smarter than his ex-partners. And now he was caught, too.

Or was he?

"Can't we talk, Cade?"

"You'll talk, Randolph, just like all your partners. Especially Brak. He's trying hard but he'll end up in the same place."

"Be like old home week when you guys get together on Mars," Janek said. "Be able to sit around telling each other how smart you were."

Randolph bit back the retort burning his tongue. He turned his full attention to Cade. "It doesn't have to be this way, Cade. I want to deal. Not talk, not information—I'm talking hard cash, Cade. I'm willing to pay up front. There's plenty of it. And I know every man has his price, Cade. Even you. I'm a practical man, always have been, I understand the way the world runs. It runs on money, Cade. Cold, hard cash. It buys and sells nations. And people..."

Randolph let his words trail off. He watched Cade as the Justice cop moved closer. There was an expression in Cade's eyes he couldn't fathom. It wasn't disinterest. It wasn't anger. Randolph watched his man, trying to read his face. Hoping that the cop was considering the offer.

"Name your price, Cade. I'm a very rich man, you understand."

"Rich enough for my terms?" Cade asked.

"Name them."

"Difficult, Randolph. I need your help. What's the going rate for a Justice cop's life? You tell me, then times it by four. Three slaughtered here in New York and one in L.A. Go ahead, Randolph. I want to hear your price."

Randolph stepped back from Cade's menacing figure. A coldness washed over him that had nothing to do with his rain-soaked clothing. It was the chill of fear, brought about by the bleak expression on Cade's face.

"Cade...I...it was Brak's man who killed them...!"

The words were hollow. They had no substance and they were wasted on T. J. Cade.

Randolph knew with shocking abruptness that he had made a bad mistake by trying to bribe the Justice cop. There was no way out left to him. No place to run, no place to hide.

He turned and slumped heavily in one of the padded couches. His eyes stared out through the canopy, seeing the city drift away as the cruiser gained height. The hazy lights vanished, replaced by the streaked leaden sky.

Janek glanced at his partner. "Braddock said it isn't over until it's finished. Remember?"

Cade nodded.

"Then I'd say it's over, Thomas. Agreed?"

"Agreed," Cade said. "Let's wrap it up, partner."

**Raw determination
in a dark new age.**

JAMES AXLER

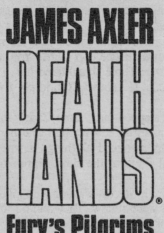

DEATHLANDS®

Fury's Pilgrims

A bad jump from a near-space Gateway leaves Ryan Cawdor and his band
of warrior survivalists in the devastated heart of the American Midwest.
In a small community that was once the sprawling metropolis of Chi-
cago, Krysty is taken captive by a tribe of nocturnal female mutants. Ryan
fears for her life, especially since she is a woman.

In the Deathlands, life is a contest where the only victor is death.

Available in January at your favorite retail outlet, or order your copy now by sending your
name, address, zip or postal code along with a check or money order (please do not send
cash) for $4.99 for each book ordered, plus 75¢ postage and handling ($1.00 in Canada),
payable to Gold Eagle Books, to:

In the U.S.	In Canada
Gold Eagle Books	Gold Eagle Books
3010 Walden Avenue	P.O. Box 609
P.O. Box 1325	Fort Erie, Ontario
Buffalo, NY 14269-1325	L2A 5X3

Please specify book title with order.
Canadian residents add applicable federal and provincial taxes.

GOLD EAGLE ®

DL-17

Gold Eagle brings another fast-paced miniseries to the action adventure front!

by PATRICK F. ROGERS

Omega Force: the last—and deadliest—option

With capabilities unmatched by any other paramilitary organization in the world, Omega Force is a special ready-reaction anti-terrorist strike force composed of the best commandos and equipment the military has to offer.

In Book 1: **WAR MACHINE**, two dozen SCUDs have been smuggled into Libya by a secret Iraqi extremist group whose plan is to exact ruthless retribution in the Middle East. The President has no choice but to call in Omega Force—a swift and lethal way to avert World War III.

WAR MACHINE, Book 1 of this three-volume miniseries, hits the retail stands in February, or order your copy now by sending your name, address, zip or postal code, along with a check or money order (please do not send cash) for $3.50, plus 75¢ postage and handling ($1.00 in Canada), payable to Gold Eagle Books, to:

In the U.S.
Gold Eagle Books
3010 Walden Avenue
P.O. Box 1325
Buffalo, NY 14269-1325

In Canada
Gold Eagle Books
P.O. Box 609
Fort Erie, Ontario
L2A 5X3

Please specify book title with your order
Canadian residents add applicable federal and provincial taxes

OM1

The year is 2030 and the world is in a state of political and territorial unrest. The Peacekeepers, an elite military force, will not negotiate for peace—they're ready to impose it with the ultimate in 21st-century weaponry.

2030
by MICHAEL KASNER

Introducing the follow-up miniseries to the WARKEEP 2030 title published in November 1992.

In Book 1: **KILLING FIELDS,** the Peacekeepers join forces with spear-throwing Zulus as violence erupts in black-ruled South Africa—violence backed by money, fanaticism and four neutron bombs.

KILLING FIELDS, Book 1 of this three-volume miniseries, hits the retail stands in March, or order your copy now by sending your name, address, zip or postal code, along with a check or money order (please do not send cash) for $3.50, plus 75¢ postage and handling ($1.00 in Canada), payable to Gold Eagle Books, to:

In the U.S.	In Canada
Gold Eagle Books	Gold Eagle Books
3010 Walden Avenue	P.O. Box 609
P.O. Box 1325	Fort Erie, Ontario
Buffalo, NY 14269-1325	L2A 5X3

Please specify book title with your order.
Canadian residents add applicable federal and provincial taxes.

GOLD EAGLE ®

WK2